INVISIBLE INKLING

EMILY JENKINS

ILLUSTRATIONS BY
HARRY BLISS

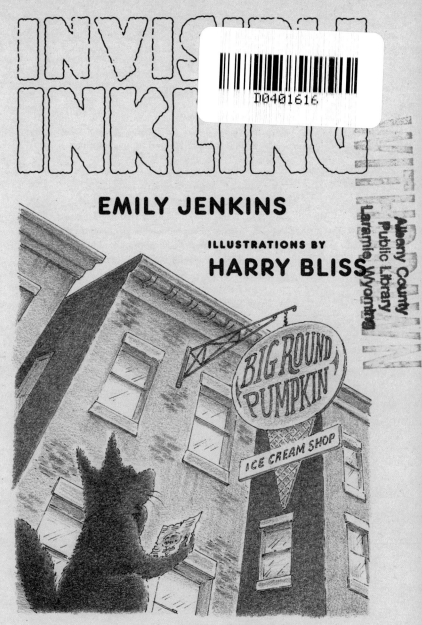

BIG ROUND PUMPKIN

ICE CREAM SHOP

BALZER + BRAY
An Imprint of HarperCollinsPublishers

For Ivy—E.J.

For Sofi—H.B.

Balzer + Bray is an imprint of HarperCollins Publishers.

Invisible Inkling
Text copyright © 2011 by Emily Jenkins
Illustrations copyright © 2011 by Harry Bliss

Library of Congress Cataloging-in-Publication Data
Jenkins, Emily, date
  Invisible Inkling / Emily Jenkins ; illustrated by Harry Bliss. — 1st ed.
     p.   cm.
  Audience: Ages 7–10.
  Summary: "When Hank Wolowitz runs into trouble in the form a of lunch-stealing
bully, he finds an unlikely ally in an invisible refugee pumpkin-loving bandapat named
Inkling"— Provided by publisher.
  ISBN 978-0-06-180222-5
  1. Bullying—Juvenile fiction. 2. Imaginary companions—Juvenile fiction.
3. Ice cream parlors—Juvenile fiction. 4. Brooklyn (New York, N.Y.)—Juvenile
fiction. [1. Bullies—Fiction. 2. Imaginary playmates—Fiction. 3. Imaginary
creatures—Fiction. 4. Ice cream parlors—Fiction. 5. Brooklyn (New York, N.Y.)—
Fiction.] I. Bliss, Harry, date. II. Title.
PZ7.J4134In 2011   2010046238
813.54—dc22   CIP
[[Fic]]   AC

Typography by Jennifer Rozbruch
16 OPM 10 9 8 7 6 5 4
❖
First paperback edition, 2012

Contents

Secret Stuff, for Serious

Hi, you.

When you're done reading this, can I ask you a favor?

Please don't tell my parents about Inkling.

And don't tell my sister Nadia, either.

Or Sasha Chin from downstairs.

Actually, please don't tell anyone that I've had an invisible bandapat living in my laundry basket for six weeks, eating my family's breakfast cereal and playing with my pop-up-book collection.

Inkling needs to stay hush-hush.

For serious.

The only reason I am telling you right now is that if I don't tell somebody, I really think my brain might explode.

And that would not be pretty.

From
Hank Wolowitz

The Fur Beneath the Sink

A thing about me is, I have an overbusy imagination. Everyone says so.

And it's true. I'm not saying I don't.

I imagine airplanes that argue with their pilots, drinks that change the color of your skin, and aliens who study human beings in science labs—all when I'm supposed to be doing something else.

Like cleaning my room.

Or listening.

But here's a thing about the invisible bandapat who's been living in my laundry basket. He is *not* imaginary.

Inkling is as real as you, or me. Or the Great Wall of China.

I know that's hard to believe. I could hardly believe it myself when I first met him.

My family is the Wolowitz family. We own an ice-cream shop a couple doors down from our apartment in Brooklyn, New York. The shop is called Big Round Pumpkin: Ice Cream for a Happy World.

The end of the summer before fourth grade, I'm hanging around the shop watching Mom, Dad, and Nadia set up for the day. That's when I first notice the bandapat.

Mom is sweeping the stoop. Nadia is kneeling on the counter in a spangly purple skirt and enormous black boots, writing on the chalkboard. Dad has just finished churning a batch of his new fall flavor, white cherry white chocolate. He's been making samples for a couple weeks, and now he's got it good enough to sell to customers. That's why Nadia is changing the flavor list that hangs over the counter.

A thing about my sister Nadia is, she has pretty handwriting.

A thing about me is, I have invented a lot of new ice-cream flavors.

Pepsi raisin chip.

Cotton-candy Gummi worm.

Poppy seed and waffle.

Sweet-potato pecan.

Don't tell me what you think. I already know most people don't like them.

My *own family* doesn't like them.

Dad makes all the ice cream himself. He invented white cherry white chocolate, nectarine swirl, and Heath bar brownie. Mom invented chocolate-covered pretzel. Nadia made up cinnamon mocha and espresso double shot.

I have invented *eight hundred* different flavors—but not a single one has ever gone up on that chalkboard.

Marshmallow peep.

Caramel popcorn.

Dried pineapple.

Cheddar-bunny crunch.

It *is* true that after saying no to every other flavor I invented, Dad whipped up an experiment batch of Cheddar-Bunny crunch earlier this summer. I told him how every kid in Brooklyn eats these Cheddar-Bunny crackers for snack. Other salty things are good in ice cream—peanuts, pistachios or pretzel bits. Why not Cheddar Bunnies?

Chin from downstairs, my best friend Wainscotting, and I—we all three spent the rest of the afternoon barfing.

That's why not Cheddar Bunnies.

Mom said could Dad please not waste time and resources making my weird ice-cream ideas any more. And he said okay.

After that, I stopped trying to help out in the shop so much. My sister works behind the counter on the weekends and in summer when it's busy, but I'm too young, and no other job is as fun as inventing ice-cream flavors.

Anyway, I first notice Inkling that day at the end of the summer in Big Round Pumpkin. There's nothing for me to do while everyone is setting up because two days ago, Wainscotting moved away to Iowa City.

Forever.

Against his will.

I don't know how I'm going to face fourth grade without him. We have been in the same class together since pre-K.

But I don't want to talk about Wainscotting. It makes my throat close up.

I want to tell you about Inkling.

It's hot that day. Sweaty, smelly, New York City Labor Day weekend hot. I open the freezer and lean my face into the cold. "Hank, please," says Mom as she puts fresh bags in the recycling bins.

I close the freezer and just lean against it.

Then I go into the kitchen and lie down on the cool tiles near the big sink.

"You're underfoot, little dude," says Dad as he makes his way from the fridge to the front of the store. He's got a large tub of ice cream under each arm.

I know I am underfoot.

But I am so, so bored.

I don't know what to *do*.

I roll over onto my stomach and press my cheek against the floor.

Oh.

There is a Lego propeller underneath the sink.

My Lego propeller that I have been looking and looking for. My City Rescue Copter can't be complete without it.

I reach for it—and my hand touches fur.

Fur.

It is so weird a feeling that I snatch my hand back.

Look around. Squint at the darkness under the sink.

Nothing furry there. Just the pipes and a bucket with a sponge in it.

I put my hand back.

Fur.

Definitely fur. Silky soft. Like—like the tail of a fluffy Persian cat.

"Ahhhhhh!" I jerk back and stand up. There is fur that I can't even see! What is happening?

I stumble as I stand and knock over a stack of metal bowls on the counter. *Bam! Caddacaddacadda*— they crash around me with a clatter. Pumpkin-colored sprinkles cascade down my legs and skid out across the floor. "Ahhhhhh!"

Dad comes rushing in. "Hank, you okay?"

"There was fur under the sink!" I yell. "I knocked the sprinkles over!"

I am feeling a little insane right now. That was so, so strange, feeling fur that wasn't there.

"What fur?" Dad asks.

"Fur! Under the sink. I felt it but I couldn't see it."

Dad looks at me. Then looks under the sink. "Little dude, I'm not seeing any fur."

"Invisible fur!"

"I cleaned under there this morning."

"But there—"

"And even if there *was* invisible fur," Dad continues, "that's no reason to make so much noise about it."

"You don't believe me!" I cry.

Dad sighs. "I believe you. It's just—can you please keep your voice down? The shop is open now. We've got customers out there."

I stand there, stupidly. The metal bowls surround me on the floor. Sprinkles are everywhere.

Of course Dad doesn't believe me.

It sounds crazy, what I'm saying.

It sounds like a goofy thing a bored kid with an over-busy imagination would invent, just to get attention.

"Sorry," I say. "I must have imagined it."

Dad almost never loses his temper. "That's okay,

Hank," he says, scratching his scraggle beard. "Just clean up the sprinkles."

He hands me the broom, but I don't use it right away. I sit down on the floor and stare at the underneath of the sink.

Either something was there, or it wasn't.

If something *was* there and I can't see it, then I need to get my eyes checked. Last year my teacher read us this book where a girl went blind on a prairie. Ever since then, I've thought it could happen to me. I could go blind, and then I'd have to work on my Lego airport purely by sense of touch and go to school with a Seeing Eye dog.

I don't know what makes a person go blind, actually. But maybe it is something like eating too much cookie-dough ice cream. In that case, I am in serious danger.

On the other hand, if nothing *was* there under the sink and yet I *felt* something, then maybe I have some nerve disease that makes my hands feel fur when really it's only tile. Bit by bit *everything* will feel furry to me. I won't be able to tell the difference between a china cup and a banana. They will both just feel like medium-size piles of fur. I will be the only person ever to have this kind of nerve problem. I'll have to drop out of school so scientists can do tests on me. I'll never learn to type or play the piano.

"Hank!" Dad is back in the kitchen, fetching a carton of milk. I can hear the espresso machine whirring outside. "I asked you to clean up the sprinkles. We can't have the kitchen floor like this. One of us could fall."

I forgot about the sprinkles. Like, I *couldn't even see them* while I was thinking about the fur. That's how my brain works.

Overbusy.

I get the dustpan. Clean up the sprinkles. Make sure every last one is gone from the kitchen floor.

Then I feel around under the sink. Nothing.

Nothing.

Pipe, tile. Bucket, sponge.

No fur.

But I am thinking: That fur was there.

I mean, I am almost sure it was really there.

It didn't *feel* like my imagination. It felt real.

We Sounded Like
Secret Agents

A thing about me and Wainscotting was, we always called each other by last names. In fact, we called *everyone* by last names, ever since we went to Science Fellow camp the summer after second grade. It was last names all the time there.

Instead of Hank, I got to be Wolowitz.

Alexander got to be Wainscotting.

We thought we sounded like secret agents.

Only, yeah.

I forgot.

I don't want to talk about Wainscotting.

I notice Inkling again the next day. During her after-noon break, Nadia convinces me to quiz her on her vocab words up in the Big Round Pumpkin overlook. She wants to know them by the start of eleventh grade because of all these tests she has to take for college. Nadia takes words and spelling very seriously. She used to win bees.

The overlook is a loft at the back of the ice-cream shop. My parents keep stuff there that they hardly ever need: holiday trim and spare parts for the machines. You climb up to it on a ladder. There's not much room to stand, but there's an old coffee table, a scrap of carpet, and a bookcase. Best, there's a window that looks out on the store from above.

From the window, you can see that the shop floor and all the lamps are pumpkin orange, but the coun-ters and tables are white. The walls have photographs of jack-o'-lanterns, blown up much larger than they are in life. The tubs of ice cream look like little spots of color in an orange and white world.

I like to guess what people will order, based on what they're wearing, how they walk, what accent they have. "What about that guy with the long hair?" I ask Nadia as she's climbing up the ladder.

She joins me at the window. "The one with the tan shorts?"

"Yeah. I think he's cinnamon mocha."

"He does look like he hangs around in coffee shops," Nadia agrees. "Those guys usually go for coffee flavors. But I think he's a vegan. He won't want any milk. So . . . raspberry sorbet."

"Raspberry is girlie," I say.

Nadia smacks me on the arm. "Flavors are not girl flavors or boy flavors."

"It's pink. Men never order pink ice cream."

"Really?"

I nod. I like to watch people. Notice things about them. It's interesting. "Lots of the regular customers always get the same thing," I tell Nadia.

"*You* always get the same thing."

That's true. I get cookie dough with chocolate sprinkles. But other people have favorites, too. "Wainscotting always got plain chocolate," I say. "Chin from downstairs gets strawberry with hot fudge. Mom, lemon sorbet."

"Dad?"

"Heath bar brownie with butterscotch sauce *and* hot

fudge, whipped cream, and a cherry on top. That's his favorite. But he likes to mix it up."

Nadia laughs. "All right, you little weirdo, quiz me on the vocab." She moves away from the window and lies down on the floor of the overlook. That's her favorite place to do serious word study.

"Okay," I say—but I don't quiz her just yet. I hold her list in my hand. I'm staring down into the shop, letting my mind go on the way it does, when—

I see a waffle cone scooting along the counter.

Not lying down and rolling, but scooting. Standing up, like it's ready for a scoop of ice cream.

Moving like it has a will of its own.

Like it just thought, Oh, I'm tired of being here in this stack with the other cones. I think I'll go for a walk down to the other end of the counter, see what's doing with the sprinkles.

Then one, two, three—

It disappears.

As if it was never there.

"Did you see that waffle cone?" I ask Nadia.

"I'm lying on the floor."

"That waffle cone was *moving*. And now it's gone."

"You and your brain," she says. "Do you know the definition of the word *hallucination*?"

"No."

"Look it up."

I check her list and read aloud, stumbling over the big words. "'Hallucination. An experience involving perception of something not present.'"

"And that means?"

"I think it means when you see something that's not there."

"Exactly," says Nadia.

"But I saw it!"

"You think you saw it," says Nadia. "That's not the same as seeing it."

"I know I saw it."

"Okay, whatever. I don't want to argue," says Nadia. "Will you quiz me on my words now?"

Attack of the French Bulldog

I try to put the fur and the waffle cone out of my mind. None of the possible explanations are pleasant to think about. Weird stuff is happening that can't be explained by the laws of nature, in which case our planet might be in store for a global meltdown full of crazy lava explosions and plagues of frogs. Or my own personal Hank Wolowitz brain has not only the nerve disease where everything feels like fur, *but also* a strange eyeball problem where things appear to move that are actually not moving and things appear to be still that are actually moving. That means I'll never drive a car, much less a helicopter, because someone with my strange sight disease and my fur-feeling problem would never be a safe driver, and in fact, I probably shouldn't even be allowed to cross the street by myself.

To take my mind off it all, I help Nadia walk Rootbeer when her shift is over. She makes extra money as a dog walker, and her main client is the French bulldog who lives across the hall from us. Seth Mnookin, our neighbor, wants Rootbeer to have a half-hour walk every day.

I actually go with Nadia pretty often, because Rootbeer is funny. She snorts when she's excited and loves to run up and down the hallways in our building, snarfling at people's doors. Mnookin says she's looking for cats, but there aren't any to find. Still, she never gives up hope.

"Hank, my man," says Nadia, when our walk is nearly finished, "will you take the leash? I have to text Max." Max is Nadia's boyfriend. He's always texting her, but he never actually comes over to our place.

"Are you gonna pay me?" I ask. "For doing your job?" I ask this every time she has me take the leash.

"No," she says, pulling out her phone. "Because I'm

still here. Supervising."

That's what she always says.

Anyway, Nadia is texting and I have the dog. We are right near Big Round Pumpkin when—

Rootbeer takes off. Dragging me behind her, she runs full speed to a tree. Skids to a stop and starts crazy barking.

There aren't any cats. Or other dogs.

There aren't any letter carriers, pretty girls, old men, people with handbags, babies in strollers, or any of the other things Rootbeer usually barks at.

Rouw! Rouw! Rootbeer howls and tries to climb the tree with her short legs.

"Does she see a squirrel?" asks Nadia, running to catch up.

We scan the trees. No squirrels.

Rootbeer takes off down the block, dragging me behind her with the leash. She skitters, knocking over garbage cans, snapping her jaws.

Nadia runs to the door of our building and holds it open. "Drag her in, Hank!" she yells. I try to pull Rootbeer inside, but the dog is racing round and round another small tree, tangling my legs in her leash. "I'm

trying," I call—but then Rootbeer lunges for the door, knocking me over. I hit the sidewalk hard and feel the leash unraveling around my legs as the dog charges. I've lost my hold on her, and Rootbeer zooms into the building, barking and drooling.

Nadia and I chase up the stairs to the fourth floor to find the dog growling at—

An empty corner of the hallway.

No cat. No squirrel.

Nothing.

"You're barking at air, loony dog," says Nadia, half laughing, half angry. She grabs Rootbeer's leash, but the dog pulls against her.

"Treats!" coaxes Nadia, straining for the door of Mnookin's apartment. "Rootbeer, I have liver treats for you inside."

The dog keeps growling at the corner.

I wave my hand through the empty space. "See, Rootbeer? It's empty"—but my hand, expecting to swing through air, hits a trembling ball of fur.

I look.

There's nothing.

Nothing I can see.

But my hand is touching something, something warm.

Fur again.

Oh, oh, oh.

There is. Something. Invisible.

Here.

This is the thing I felt under the sink. Only now, trembling in the corner.

The thing that ate the waffle cone.

It has to be.

That thing is here. Terrified 'cause Rootbeer wants to kill it.

My head spins. The dog's drooling jaws are just a foot away.

Instinctively, I stroke the soft fur of the invisible thing.

It is lost, probably.

The creature's small forepaws reach up and grip my wrist, and I bend down, saying loudly, "Nothing here, see, Rootbeer? Don't bark at the air."

The invisible thing climbs nimbly into my arms and wraps its front legs around my neck. I hold its warm, frightened body, trying to look like I am doing nothing much with my hands.

I kick the air of the corner where the creature has been sitting. "Nothing," I say again. "Silly dog."

Nadia pulls on Rootbeer's leash and reaches her key toward Seth Mnookin's apartment door, but suddenly the dog isn't lunging at the corner. She's coming at me. I back up as the invisible creature hugs me, heavy and shaking with terror.

"Save me," it whispers in my ear.

I'm so shocked, I nearly fall down.

It can speak.

English.

The invisible creature claws my neck in fear, and I stumble back against the wall. "Put

Rootbeer in Seth's apartment," I tell Nadia. "Quick."

Nadia bends down and grabs Rootbeer around the middle like you would a bag of potatoes. The dog wiggles and strains, running her short legs in the air and growling.

Nadia manages to get the door to Mnookin's apartment open. She tosses Rootbeer in.

I can hear the dog's nails skitter on the floor as she lands. She lunges to get back out, but Nadia slams the door and leans against it.

Rootbeer barks and doesn't stop.

Not Actually a
Big Round Pumpkin

While Nadia fluffs up her drooping hair in our bathroom, I go to my room. I set the invisible creature gently on the pillow of my bed. There's a slight dent where it's sitting, but otherwise I can't tell it's even there.

"You okay?"

I feel strange speaking to the air, but the creature answers right away. "Alive!" it cries in a hoarse but energetic voice. "Alive, alive, alive!"

"Yeah," I say, in wonder. "You are."

"Alive!"

I can't believe this is happening. I have a rush of questions. "Are you hurt? Did Rootbeer bite you? Do you need a Band-Aid?"

And: "Why can't I see you? What kind of creature are you?"

And: "You're a boy, right? You sound like a boy."

And: "Are there lots of your kind all over Brooklyn and we just don't know it? How do you make yourself invisible?"

The creature ignores everything. "Let me tell you this," he says. "I owe you, big-time. You saved my life."

"Can you appear and disappear? What do you look like? Are you bleeding? Are you even real?"

"Of course I'm real," the creature snaps. "We're having a conversation, aren't we?"

"Yes, but—"

"No buts. I'm here. I'm real. Get used to it. What's your name?"

"Wolowitz. I mean, my first name is Hank, but I'd rather you call me Wolowitz.

"Wolowitz! I'm Inkling."

Wow.

I am having a conversation with an invisible animal.

A normal conversation, just like I'd have with a human.

I wish Wainscotting was here for this.

"Is Inkling your first name or your last?" I ask.

"It's my *name*," he says. "Lots of people have just one name."

"Only pop stars."

Inkling changes the subject. "What you did for me just now, Wolowitz? Fantastic. A heroic rescue. I am in your debt."

"It wasn't much," I say. "Anyone would have done it."

"Are you kidding? It was life or death with that—what did you call it?"

"Rootbeer," I say.

"It was life or death with that rootbeer," says Inkling. "I'm in your debt until I can return the favor. We bandapats have a code of honor."

"Is that what you are?" I reach out. My hand connects with soft fur, though I still can't see anything. I run my palm gently along Inkling's back. "You're a bandapat?"

"A little-known mammal native only to the Peruvian Woods of Mystery," Inkling explains. "We are extremely cute but naturally invisible, which helps our species survive in the fearsome woods among predators and other scary stuff."

"And you speak English?"

"Of course," he says. "And Yiddish. And Mandarin. All bandapats do. Only there aren't very many of us. We are endangered. I am the only one in Brooklyn. Possibly even in North America."

"But why did you come *here*?" I ask. "I mean, with dogs and all that, I don't imagine it's very safe for you."

"Bandapats eat squash," Inkling explains. "We can eat almost anything, actually, but we *need* the squash because we need lots of vitamin A. What's more, it's really, really yummy."

"Squash?"

"We prefer pumpkin, but we like butternut, too. Or

acorn. Most any kind that's not zucchini," says Inkling.

"Back to why you came here."

"Oh. Where I come from, among the Ukrainian glaciers—"

I interrupt: "I thought you said Peruvian Woods of Mystery."

Inkling ignores me. "—there developed a shortage. All the squash growing among the glaciers was harvested by humans to cook into pies and serve with turkey." He sighs.

"The last of my kind began to waste away for want of it. There were so few of us, so few—and finally, there was only me."

Even though he's for-serious lying—hello? there are no squash growing in glacier ice—I like his stories. He probably has an overbusy imagination, too. Plus, I feel a wave of sadness for Inkling.

He's all alone, in a world that can't even see him.

There's nobody like him for miles, even continents, around.

"Why come to Brooklyn for squash?" I ask. "I mean, we have squash, you can get it in the stores, but it's not, like, the squash capital of the planet or anything."

"Ahh," says Inkling, sounding excited. "There may be *more* squash elsewhere on the planet, but here in Brooklyn, you have *bigger* squash."

"We do?"

"The biggest! I was looking for it when the rootbeer attacked me. Here in Brooklyn, you have the big round pumpkin."

"You mean my family's shop?"

The springs of the bed creak, and the pillow squishes up and down. I think Inkling is jumping. "Your family *owns* the big round pumpkin?"

"Yes."

"Oh, this is news. Good, good news. You can't imagine, Wolowitz, how far I traveled with that small bit of newspaper, that bit with the ad showing the pumpkin. Giving the address where I could find it. It was in an old issue of the *New York Times* food section that somebody threw out. Just luck that I read it, but as soon as I did, I felt like the pumpkin was calling me. I had a purpose. A destiny!"

He must be leaning forward, as I can feel his warm bandapat breath on my face.

"I am starved for squash. Haven't had it in months. I came miles and miles and miles to get here. I camped out in people's hatchbacks, on trains, planes, underneath seats in cross-country buses. I slept on park benches and underneath cars. All to get to that big round pumpkin—but when I got here, I couldn't find it."

"I saw you in the shop," I say. "I saw you eat that waffle cone, and I think I grabbed you by accident under the kitchen sink."

"That was you?" Inkling chuckles. "Sorry, I didn't recognize you. All humans kind of look alike to me, honestly."

"That's okay."

"I've been searching the shop for days now. There are pictures of pumpkins, sure, pictures aplenty; but your parents are hiding the *actual* pumpkin really well. I've been all over that place and I haven't found it. Can you help me?"

"But you did find it," I explain. "It's an ice-cream shop named after a pumpkin."

"I want the pumpkin!" Inkling shouts. The bed bounces. "I *need* that big round pumpkin!"

"I am sorry," I say. "But the big round pumpkin is a

symbol of the earth. It's not an *actual* pumpkin."

"You're kidding me." The bouncing stops.

"No."

"It's a symbol."

"Yes."

"Of the earth."

"Yes."

"Oh." His voice sounds choked and sad.

I realize that wherever he's traveled from, Inkling has come a long, long way. Now he's learned that the thing he came for—the pumpkin he thought was his destiny—doesn't exist.

There's a snuffle from the bed, and I can tell he is crying.

Theft of Cheesy Goodness

"Do you want to get some pizza?" I ask gently. Pizza is the food I always want when I'm feeling alone.

"Yes, please," says Inkling, sniffing. "What's pizza?"

"Crust and tomato sauce and cheesy goodness," I say.

"Can you really eat it? Or is it just a symbol of something else?"

"You can really eat it," I promise.

"Then let's go."

He climbs onto my back. Nadia takes us to Giardini's for a small pie, since my parents have to work through dinner anyway.

At the pizza place, Inkling sits under my chair. My plan is to rip off bits and give them to him where nobody can see, the way you would a dog—but after his first bite, Inkling starts poking my leg hard, under the table.

I poke him back.

He pokes me again. "Cheesy goodness," he whispers. "More cheesy goodness."

I rip him off a bigger piece and sneak it down.

It's gone in two seconds, with a small slurping noise.

"More." He pokes me again. "More cheesy goodness."

Nadia stands to get a shaker of oregano and some napkins. As soon as her back is turned, Inkling climbs onto the table—I can hear him huffing—and starts pulling the rest of our pie toward him.

"Excuse me!" I grab the crust and pull it back. "You can't take the whole thing!"

Several bites disappear from one edge. I see them

go invisible as they enter Inkling's mouth, a string of cheese hanging in midair before he slurps it up.

"Come on!" I say.

"Cheesy goodness," he mumbles, between bites. "Inkling likes the cheesy goodness."

"You're going to have to get off the table as soon as Nadia comes back," I whisper.

"Now then!" he says. "Cheesy goodness!" The entire pie starts scooting across the table again.

"No!" I reach for it, but Inkling's too fast. The pizza flops onto the floor and zips across the tile, under two tables and several chairs, around a cooler full of drinks, and into the darkest corner of Giardini's.

In seconds, it is gone.

All that's left is the slices on our plates.

"Hank, my man," says Nadia, returning. "Way to hog the pizza. You eat that fast, you'll make yourself sick, you know."

"It wasn't me," I say. "It was—"

She squints her eyes at me. "It was *what*? Your invisible friend?"

I start laughing, because it's true. And my life has become so strange and so happy so quickly that I can't stop. I laugh and laugh until Nadia has to hit me on the back and make me drink a glass of water.

At home that night, Inkling tells me I have to keep him secret. Over the years, humans have endangered bandapats by trapping them and locking them in hush-hush science labs. The scientists are searching for the source of bandapat invisibility, but it's never been found. And in the labs, the bandapats waste away and die from sadness. "Promise me you won't say a word, Wolowitz," Inkling begs. "Because I can't have that happen to me. I can't be a science experiment. It would break me."

I promise, and tell him we also have to keep him secret because of Mom's "no pets" policy. "Never, never" is the rule. She says seven hundred books, two kids, and

Dad all together in our apartment—that's already more than she can handle.

We shake hands on it, Inkling and I. It is strange shaking hands with an invisible creature. His paw is rough on the bottom and divided into pads.

What does he look like?

Fluffy.

Stout.

Soft ears, a large tail, and padded feet with hard little claws.

That's all I can tell, so far.

Maybe he'll tell me more, later. Maybe he'll let me touch his face.

While Mom, Dad, and Nadia are on the living room couch watching *E.T.* that night, I make Inkling a bed in my laundry basket. I feed him a bowl of cereal and some leftover broccoli for dinner. "That rootbeer didn't hurt me any worse than a kangaroo I fought once," he says, munching.

"You fought a kangaroo?"

"Oh, they're all over the outback of Ethiopia," Inkling says. "I dropped on one that was hopping home with a huge, yummy-looking pumpkin. Waited in a tree and just dropped when the roo was least expecting it. There was big-time combat. She defended her pumpkin to the very last. But in the end, no bloodshed. Just aches and pains."

Of course he's for-serious lying—hello? Kangaroos don't come from Ethiopia, and last time he mentioned home it was in the Ukraine—but it's more fun to listen to him than to call him on it.

"Who ate the pumpkin finally?" I ask.

"Me, of course. Bandapats nearly always win in combat. Invisibility gives us an advantage."

I can't resist saying, "Except maybe with dogs, huh?"

"What?"

"Dogs, and their sense of smell. They can always tell where you are."

"I don't know what you're talking about."

"Rootbeer!" I say. "She can tell exactly where you are. Even when you're up in a tree."

"The rootbeer's not a dog," says Inkling.

"Yes, she is."

"Listen, I have traveled all over the world, and I've seen dogs and dogs and dogs. This rootbeer is nothing like a dog. Her face is all squashed in and she has ears like a bat."

I laugh.

"I'm fine with dogs," Inkling claims, "but the root-beer is another story. I have to steer clear of *her*." He eats another piece of broccoli. "Anyway, I'm only sticking around until the Hetsnickle is paid."

"Hetsnickle?"

"Hetsnickle was a famous bandapat. The debt of honor is named after her. You know, how I have to save your life because you saved me from that rootbeer? That's the Hetsnickle debt."

I nod, but I'm not thinking about the Hetsnickle. What I'm really thinking is:

I have an invisible friend.
It is not my imagination.
It is true, real life.
I have an invisible friend.

Get Some Squash
in That Thing

In the early morning, before anyone else is up, I give Inkling a tour of the Wolowitz apartment. Dad's seven hundred books, spilling off the shelves and piled on the floor. Nadia's stash of cosmetics and hair products. The TV, the big worn sectional couch, Mom's plants, and the photograph of me and Nadia when I was just a baby, blown up larger than life and hanging in the dining area.

"You got squash in that thing?" Inkling wants to know as I show him the refrigerator.

"I doubt it."

"Why not?"

"No one in my family likes squash."

"You don't like squash?"

"Nah."

"That's completely insane," says Inkling. "I swear, I will never understand human beings."

"You can eat breakfast cereal or bread or leftovers," I say. "But if you eat something special like strawberries or chocolate milk, my mom might notice." I pour some Oatie Puffs onto the kitchen counter for him and set out a dish of almonds.

"Thanks," he says. "But see if you can get some squash in that thing. I can't stick around if there isn't going to be squash."

"I'll try," I tell him—but then I don't think much more about it. Tomorrow is the first day of school. I notice Mom has put my backpack on the kitchen counter alongside a stack of folders and notebooks, plus the pencil case I picked out.

The first day of fourth grade.

Without Wainscotting.

Who will I sit with at lunch?

Who will I play with at recess?

"Do you miss your friends?" I ask Inkling. "I mean, your fellow bandapats in the Woods of Mystery or wherever?"

"Sure."

"Do you write to them?"

"No."

"How come? Don't bandapats write?"

"We write."

"So why don't you write to them?"

"I don't choose to discuss it."

"What?"

"I don't choose to discuss it."

"Don't choose to discuss what?" I persist. "Writing?"

"I told you before, Wolowitz. Bandapats are an endangered species."

Oh.

I feel like a jerk now. But he's said so many different things, I haven't known what to believe.

"I'm sorry," I say.

There's no answer. Several Oatie Puffs disappear from the kitchen counter.

"Did you have a best friend?" I ask. "Someone you miss in particular?"

At first, he doesn't answer. "I was very popular," says Inkling finally. "Let's leave it at that."

"Come with me tomorrow," I blurt out. "Come see what school is like."

"What? No way."

"You shouldn't sit lonely at home all day," I coax. "Plus, you know all about popularity. That would be a big help to me, actually, since my best friend moved away. You could give me advice."

"Not happening," Inkling says.

"Why not?"

"I hate crowds. Especially crowds of children. They're dangerous for an invisible person." Inkling makes a shivering noise. "All those feet."

"Please?"

"If it's a matter of life and death, I'll come," says Inkling. "Because of the Hetsnickle. Otherwise, I want to stay home and look at your pop-up books."

"Come on, you'll like it!" I say, even though I know that isn't true.

"Is your life in danger?" Inkling demands.

"No," I have to admit.

"Will there be squash at school?"

"No."

"Will there be pizza?"

"Only on pizza Fridays."

"Then this conversation is over," Inkling says.

I hear a thump as he leaps from the kitchen counter to the floor. Then a soft *pat-pat* as he pads out of the room.

I think about following him, but I don't.

The thought of facing fourth grade alone just makes me paralyzed or something.

There Is No Partial Credit

At school, the good news is that Sasha Chin from downstairs is in my class. When she sees me come into the room, she bangs a rhythm on the table where she's sitting.

Bam bam! Dada bam bam!

I'm hanging up my backpack, but I bang the same rhythm back on the wall behind my hook. *Bam bam! Dada bam bam!*

It's a thing we do sometimes.

The bad news is that Locke, Linderman, and Daley are here, too. They're these girls Chin likes to hang around with. Them being in our class means that more than half the time Chin will be in girlie land—and not with me.

They're, like, her official friends.

I'm just the kid from her building she hangs out with.

Our teacher, Ms. Cherry, has complicated hair and wears very high heels. "Strangers are friends you haven't gotten to know yet," she announces, in one of those fake teacher voices, high and jolly. "That's our motto for the start of this year. Friends are flowers in the garden of life. Let's plant an imaginary friendship flower bed together, here in our classroom!"

I don't think Ms. Cherry would understand about me and Chin being building friends but not official friends. Still, the day is going okay, for a first-ever school day without Wainscotting. We meet the new science teacher, who has a lab with frogs and giant hissing cockroaches. And we get to tell about our summer vacations.

I think my summer is going to sound boring, because all I did was hang out in Big Round Pumpkin week after week, but Linderman and Daley have lots of questions about the shop and how we make the ice cream. So I feel kinda good, knowing the answers.

Everything is really all right—until gym class.

I have never been able to pay attention in gym. No matter what we're doing, my mind gets going with ideas that have nothing to do with sports. Today we're starting a soccer unit, and when the teacher is talking about halfbacks and midfielders and wingers and strikers, I think about how Nadia told me that if I went in her room again, she'd scoop my eyeballs out with a teaspoon and flush them down the toilet.

I wonder if you can really truly do that kind of eyeball scooping, or whether eyeballs are actually difficult to remove from their sockets.

If they *were* easy to get out, wouldn't eyeballs pop out by accident all the time? And sometimes you'd just see one lying on a counter in a public bathroom, or on the street, like you do candy wrappers?

That *never* happens. You never see eyeballs lying around.

So they *must* be hard to get out.

Kaminski, the gym teacher, takes us out into the big schoolyard. She divides us and kids from Mr. Hwang's class into several teams. I'm on a team called the Pink Floyds. Our opposite team is the Foo Fighters.

"Scrimmage!" Kaminski yells, and blows her whistle.
We play.

I am being a midfielder or something like that. I don't really know what's going on, but I'm trying to fake it, running in the same direction as other kids who are Pink Floyds.

Suddenly, someone yells my name. "Hank! Go!"

A ball is flying through the air.

It's coming at me.

Oh! I've got it.

I've actually got control of it.

I am going pretty fast. Down the court to the Pink Floyd goal.

A surge of joy spreads through me. I *own* that ball! People are cheering.

I kick the ball as hard as I can into the net.

Bam!

It's in!

I'm breathing hard, but it feels great, making that goal. Amazing.

Kaminski blows her whistle. She has been blowing it for quite a while, I think, and with a rush I realize: Something is wrong.

The other kids are not cheering.

They are yelling.

Mean yelling.

"What was that?" A big kid called Gillicut looms over me. He's in Mr. Hwang's class.

"I made a goal," I squeak.

Gillicut points at the net. "What goal is that?" he barks.

"Pink Floyd," I say. "I mean, I know which is my team's goal. I may not be a soccer dude, but I'm far from stupid."

"Yeah, Spanky," Gillicut sneers. "That *is* the Pink Floyd goal."

"The name is Hank," I say. "You are mispronouncing it, a little."

"Pink Floyds put balls in the *Foo Fighter* goal," says Gillicut. "Foo Fighters put balls in the Pink Floyd goal."

Oh.

Drat.

"Sorry," I say. And I really am. "But the ball did go straight in," I add cheerfully. "Maybe our team could get partial credit?"

"There is no partial credit!" screams Gillicut. He

sounds like he really, really cares about soccer. "You messed up the whole game."

"Sorry," I say again.

His huge Gillicut face is right on top of mine, and I'm scared he might actually murder me, he seems so mad.

Kaminski blows her whistle. "Break it up, boys. Sportsmanship, remember?"

Gillicut steps away. "Later, Spankitty Spankpants."

"Later what?" I ask, my legs shaking.

"I. Will. See. You. Later," he says.

The Invention of Wood Erk

"Let me understand this soccer thing," Inkling says. "I saw it once on television."

I told him all about what happened at school the minute I got home. Now we're sitting on the couch. I'm messing with one of my Lego helicopters, trying to get the doors to stay on right. But I'm not really concentrating.

"You find yourself a bunch of friends and buy a small pumpkin," Inkling continues.

"No, you don't."

"Then you hack off the stem, save that to eat later,

and paint it black and white."

"No, no."

"And you kick it—what? Until it smashes? The winner is the one who smashes the pumpkin?"

"No, no, no!"

"Does he get to eat it all by himself? Or does everyone share the pumpkin at the end?"

"It's not a pumpkin. It's a soccer ball."

"Oh." I can hear him scratching his ear with his back paw—*thump, thump, thump*—like a dog. "A ball. Really?" he finally asks.

"Really."

"And you're smashing it with your feet? I really don't see the point of this game."

"You're getting it all wrong!" I say. "It goes like this—"

But then I shut my mouth.

Today's events have made it painfully clear that I don't understand soccer, either. "Gillicut hates me," I moan. "That's the real point of the story."

"But I like you," says Inkling. "I'm invisible! I can speak three languages. I am way cooler than Gillicut. So who cares?"

I say, "He said 'See. You. Later' in that way that

means 'See you later to rip your tongue out of your head, shorty.'"

"Listen." Inkling leans against me on the couch. "You took down that fierce rootbeer unarmed. You rescued an innocent bandapat from harm and asked for nothing in return. No way are you scared of some guy who's working himself up just because you kicked a black-and-white ball in the wrong direction."

I pet Inkling's soft fur, scratching his neck the way he likes.

"I might, though," I say. "I might actually be *very* scared of that guy."

"Who are you talking to, little dude?" Dad asks.

I jump.

I thought Inkling and I were alone in the living room, but here is Dad, standing in front of me. His hair is sticking up, and there's a dribble of chocolate ice cream on his white shirt.

Hmm. Who am I talking to? "I—I have an imaginary friend," I lie.

"Oh, wow." Dad plops himself on the couch next to me.

On top of Inkling.

Oh no!

My dad is pretty big. He could squish Inkling for serious.

"Erk," Inkling moans.

"I used to have an imaginary friend," says Dad, leaning back and putting his arm around me. "Back when I was your age."

"Erk."

"Is that your friend's name?" Dad asks. "Erk?"

"Yes," I say. "Um, Dad? Would you mind standing up?"

"My friend's name was Gary," says Dad. "Good old Gary. I called him Gary 'cause I thought it was a cowboy name. He used to have a horse and

everything. He really helped me out during some lonely times. Hey! I bet you're feeling lonely with Alexander gone to Iowa City."

"Erk."

"Erk is an unusual name, though. How did you come up with it?"

"Dad—"

"It must be his last name, though, am I right? 'Cause you call everyone by last names. So what's his first?"

"Would you move?"

"Wood Yoomove Erk, that's his name?" Dad laughs. "I love the way your mind works, little dude."

"Dad!" I shout. "Stand up!"

"Okay." Dad scratches his head and stands. "Oh no! I was sitting on Erk, wasn't I?"

"Yes!"

Dad bends over and looks at the empty spot where he was sitting. I can't tell if Inkling is there or not. "I'm sorry, Erk," he says, slow and sweet. "I'll be more careful in future."

I roll my eyes. "Don't talk to him like he's a baby, Dad. Sheesh." (For a moment I've forgotten that Wood Erk doesn't exist, not even in my imagination.)

Dad pats my shoulder. "Look, I know Erk is probably kind of a private thing. I won't talk to him any more or ask you questions. Why don't we just watch some TV together? I don't have to start cooking dinner for another half hour."

I feel the couch next to me. Inkling is gone.

"Thanks, Dad," I say. "That would be great."

I hope Inkling's okay.

"Can I sit down again now?" Dad asks.

"Sure," I tell Dad. "Right here."

Dad plops back down with a sigh and flips on the TV. Food channel. That's what he always picks.

"Dad?" I ask, after a minute of watching this gray-haired lady make meat loaf. "When you were a kid, were you good at sports?"

I'm thinking he'll say no. I've never seen him play a sport in my life.

I actually *want* him to say no.

"I was good at Hacky Sack in college," Dad answers.

"What's Hacky Sack?"

"You stand in a circle, and everyone keeps a beanbag up in the air using only their feet."

"Did people ever get all mad and stuff if you, like,

failed to keep the beanbag up in the air?"

Dad flexes a muscle. "Not at me. I was the Hacky Sack master."

"So they didn't want to—I don't know—*see you later* and rip your tongue out of your head 'cause you messed up?"

"No way." Dad laughs. "I ruled that little beanbag."

Oh.

I decide not to tell him what happened in gym class today.

Sprinkie Tax

The next day, in the cafeteria, I'm just sitting down to eat when Gillicut stalks over. He demands that I show him the contents of my lunch box. "Spanky Pantalones!" he shouts. "Whatcha got?"

I remember the way he came at me in gym. I remember how he said "See. You. Later."

I open my lunch box and show him.

"Bread and peanut butter, yuck," he says. "Yogurt, yuck. Apple, yuck. Oh, Oreos!"

"They're not Oreos. They're organic sandwich cookies," I mumble, hoping he'll drop them.

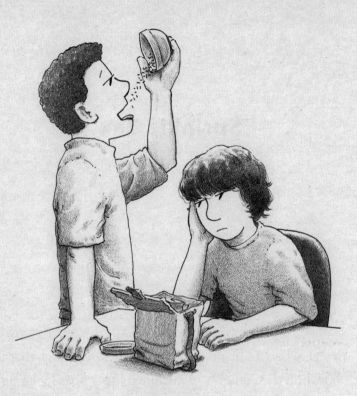

But no. He just eats them both at once and grabs my Tupperware container full of chocolate sprinkles.

"These are mine, too," he says, mouth full. "How come ya got sprinkies?"

"Sprinkles?" I say. "My parents own an ice-cream store."

"You get sprinkies every day?" Gillicut asks.

"A lot of days, I guess."

Why am I telling the truth? I think. *I should be lying right now.*

But it's too late. Gillicut pours the sprinkles into his mouth. He tosses the empty Tupperware on the floor, then trots across the room to the lunch line.

My shoulders sink and my eyes fill.

I find the Tupperware over by a garbage can and pick it up. When I get back to my table, Chin is there. "Spanky Pantalones?" she says, laughing. "I heard that."

I can't believe she's laughing. That guy just took all my dessert.

I don't answer her. Just keep myself busy opening my yogurt and finding my spoon.

Blueberry yogurt. Blueberry yogurt.

That's my favorite, and if I just think about that, I won't cry in front of everyone.

Chin watches me.

"Sorry," she says after a minute of me not answering her. "For laughing." She breaks off half of her chocolate-chip granola bar and pushes it across the table to me. "Since he took your cookies."

"Thanks."

We eat for a while.

I have the granola bar first, in case Gillicut returns.

Chin eats an apple-butter-and-pickle sandwich, like she does every day.

Then she bangs a rhythm on the table. *Bam dada bam! Dada bim bam bang!*

I'm still a little mad at her for laughing, but I bang the same rhythm back.

"You know what we should build after the Great Wall of China?" Chin asks. (We are building a Great Wall of China from matchsticks, when there's nothing else to do.)

"What?"

"Taj Mahal. Taj Mahal would be slam-bang."

And for a second, I think: Maybe fourth grade won't be so bad without Wainscotting.

Maybe it'll be good, even.

But then Gillicut is back, setting his tray of garbage on our table. "Did yah cry 'cause you lost your sprinkies, Spanky Baby?"

"No."

"Good thing. 'Cause now you've got a sprinkie tax."

"What?"

"Sprinkie tax goes like this," Gillicut says, speaking

slowly as if I'm dumb. "Every day, you bring me sprinkies in your lunch box. Only, not the chocolate ones. I want rainbow."

"Hank doesn't *live* at Big Round Pumpkin," says Chin. "He doesn't have rainbow *sprinkles,* like, sitting in his refrigerator."

We do have sprinkles sitting in our refrigerator, actually. Dad is a big one for late-night ice-cream feasts, especially when he's trying to invent new flavors. But I keep this to myself.

"So? He can get them, easy." Gillicut yanks the neck of my T-shirt back so it's tight against my throat.

I choke, my breath comes in gulps—

But Gillicut releases my shirt before the lunch aides have time to notice what he's doing. Then he takes his tray and dumps his trash in front of me. A pile of paper napkins, a Styrofoam plate full of unwanted baked beans, a banana peel, an oozing milk carton. All on top of my lunch.

I think: if I throw out Gillicut's garbage today, I'm probably going to be doing it every day for the rest of the school year.

Every day. Touching his slimy baked-bean garbage

and his used paper napkins. "Throw it *out*, Spankitty Spankpants!" Gillicut bends over and whispers. "Throw it out or I'll rip your ears off and feed them to the science-lab hamsters."

He grabs the oozing garbage from the table and shoves it into my arms.

Fourth grade isn't going to be good after all.

The Big Fur Fluff-Up

"I know what you should do," Inkling says. "You should bite Gillicut on the ankle."

"There's no biting allowed at school."

"I bet there's no sprinkle stealing allowed, either."

"That's true."

"The trick is to chomp down really hard on the ankle with both the top and bottom teeth. Then waggle your head around to make it hurt more."

I sigh.

"Come on."

I sigh again.

"I can tell you're not going to bite him," says Inkling. "I can tell by your voice."

"I don't think I can."

"Then the least you can do is fluff up your fur to make yourself look bigger."

I laugh. "What?"

"A big fur fluff-up is very scary to an opponent."

"I don't have fur."

"On your head you do."

"That's hair."

"So fluff it up. Gillicut will back right down once you show him how really fluffy you can get. You can use some of Nadia's volumizer putty."

"Volumizer what?"

"Putty. That stuff she puts in her hair that makes it stand up. She's got it on the bathroom counter."

"Fluffing my hair is not going to make Gillicut back down. It's just going to get me in trouble with Nadia."

I don't add that no boys have fluffy hair at Public School 166.

"This isn't the jungle," I tell Inkling. "It's the lunchroom."

"Same thing."

"Fluffy is different for humans."

"Suit yourself," says Inkling. "But I'm telling you it's worth a try."

In the morning I find Nadia's volumizer putty and scoop some into a plastic bag.

"Put more," says Inkling.

I jump. I didn't know he was in the bathroom with me.

"You shouldn't come into the bathroom with people," I say. "People like privacy in the bathroom."

"You're just stealing volumizer putty," says Inkling.

"I know, but—"

"Whatever. I swear, I will never understand human beings."

"Just don't come into the bathroom unless the door's open, okay?"

"Got it. Now go on. Put more in. You want to get a really big fluff-up."

I put more in.

Right before lunch I go to the boys' room at school and mush the putty through my hair until it stands on end all over my head.

I look insane. I know I do. But maybe insane is good, you know? Maybe insane is what it takes to scare away someone like Gillicut.

Entering the cafeteria, I turn my neck side to side, displaying my fur fluff as Inkling taught me. I keep my shoulders low and my gaze fierce. It's a display of size and health, and it's supposed to make your enemies back down.

"Spikey Spankopolis. You been to the beauty parlor?" Gillicut comes up from behind.

"No," I say, with great seriousness. "I have not."

"Did the beauty-parlor lady stick your finger in an electric socket?" he asks. "Or did you see your own ugly face in the mirror, and now you can't live down the shock?"

"No," I say again. I can tell the fluff isn't working, but I try to see the plan through to the end. Inkling promised it would work if I'd just commit myself and not wimp out. "I have bigger hair than you, Gillicut," I say loudly. "In fact, your hair is small and weak looking, compared to mine."

He bursts into a fit of giggles. Pointing at me.

Soon a number of other kids are pointing and laughing, too.

Drat.

I should never have listened to Inkling. He thinks the laws of the lunchroom are the same as the laws of the Ethiopian Outback, but clearly:

They. Are. Not.

Gillicut holds his hand out to me. "Sprinkie tax, Spikey Spank."

I give him my Tupperware of sprinkles.

I brought the rainbow kind. Just in case.

Gillicut leaves his hand out and gets my dried-fruit snack.

And then my chocolate milk.

Instead of eating what's left, I run to the boys' room and wash the putty out of my hair.

Every day after that, regular as regular, Gillicut takes whatever's best in my lunch.

The Squash Situation Becomes Desperate

Inkling and I settle into a happy routine. At least, it makes me happy. We get up early and watch science videos while eating breakfast cereal. He leans against my leg while we watch, telling me wild stories about bandapat life in Ethiopia, or the Woods of Mystery, or wherever he's supposed to be from.

Sure, he's a liar, but at least he's never boring.

When the rest of my family wakes up, Inkling climbs onto a high shelf in the kitchen and watches us as we eat and talk and get ready for the day. Every now and then I toss him up an Oatie Puff and he eats it in midair.

In the afternoons we play Monopoly or Blokus in my room, and I tell him everything that's going on.

Even more than I used to tell Wainscotting.

"I can probably figure out a new plan to defeat Gillicut," says Inkling, the day after the hair fluff. "But the thing is, I need some squash. I haven't had any for ages and ages."

"I know," I tell him. "I'll get you some."

But finding squash is not so easy. Like I said, no

one in my family eats it. My allowance is two dollars a week, but all of that goes to paying Mom back for my Lego airport, which cost a lot. I never see any cash, and Nadia won't pay me for helping with the dog walking.

"I need the squash, Wolowitz," Inkling says. "I'm in a weakened state. My bandapat instincts are dulled. You saw how the rootbeer nearly ate me. And your dad sat on me, too."

I nod.

"Get me squash," he says. "Get me squash or I can't stay here anymore." Then, coaxing: "Get me squash and I can solve your Gillicut problem."

"When do you need it by?" I ask.

"Yesterday!" cries Inkling. "But today will do."

So we try. He climbs onto my back, and we go down-stairs to Chin's apartment. "Hello," I say, when Chin opens the door. "Do you have any squash I can borrow?"

Chin laughs. She is wearing a tutu. I have never seen her dressed that way before. "I don't think so," she answers. "Mom, do we have squash?"

Chin's mom comes up. "No squash. Tell your dad I'm sorry, Hank."

"It's not for my dad."

"Then what's it for?" Chin wants to know.

Locke and Linderman appear at the door. They are wearing tutus also.

Suddenly I can't think of a reasonable answer.

"I didn't know you had friends over," I say to Chin. "I'll see you later."

"Do you want to come in?" she asks. "We're doing a ballet and we could totally use a prince."

"That's okay."

"There could be a sword fight if you want. It doesn't have to be leaping around or romance or anything."

"No, no," I say. "Hello, Dahlia. Hello, Emma. I have to look for squash now."

I turn and run up the stairs.

"Keep trying," says Inkling.

"But that was a disaster," I say.

"Keep trying," he repeats. "I need the squash."

We knock at Seth Mnookin's, but only Rootbeer is home. She barks like a crazy dog when she smells Inkling on the other side of the door.

"Nadia?" I ask my sister, back in the apartment. "Will you buy me a squash? It'll only cost maybe four dollars, and I'll pay you back when I'm done paying Mom for the Lego airport."

"Nuh-uh," says Nadia, not even looking up from her book. "You're gonna be owing on that airport for, like, two years."

"Come on," I beg. "Just one little squash."

"No way," says Nadia. "You never paid me back when I bought you those waffle cookies. Or when I fronted you money for the helicopter pop-up book."

She's right.

"I'm sorry," I tell Inkling, when we're alone in my room again.

"But I need it," he says. "Need my squash, so bad."

"No one has it," I say. "And I don't have any money."

"I'm sluggish," he moans. "I'm losing fur in patches. You've gotta help me, Wolowitz. Otherwise how can *I* help you?"

I can hear the desperation in his voice.

I want to help. I really do.

The question is, how?

I Am Not an Ambassador
of Goodwill

No squash, no solution from Inkling. Over the next week, Gillicut gets not only five Tupperwares of rainbow sprinkles—one each day—but a nectarine, two bags of sandwich cookies, a bag of Cheddar Bunnies, a yogurt drink, pretzels, raspberries, a Luna bar, and a box of dried cranberries.

The Monday after, Chin convinces me I should I talk to the lunch aides.

"Don't tattle," says the old, blind lady. "You boys work it out."

"Tell him not to," says the bored lady in the sunglasses.

"Tell him I'm writing his name down," says the cranky lady with the orange hair.

But writing his name down doesn't help. Gillicut is on a rampage. And he's not dumb: He kicks under the table, pinches while he's smiling, and never makes a move until the aides are busy with someone else.

Tuesday, I talk to my dad about the problem, when he's reading to me before bed.

"There must be a peaceable solution to this conflict, little dude," he says. "Can you think of a peaceable solution?"

I shake my head.

Dad sighs. He's a pacifist, which means he doesn't believe in war, karate lessons, or toy guns. "Did you try saying 'Please leave me alone'?" he asks.

"Yes."

"Did you try saying 'Back off'?"

"Yes."

"But the guy didn't back off?"

"No."

"Oh, little dude," my dad says. "That's rough."

"I know," I say. He takes my hand and squeezes.

"Let me think on it," he says.

Wednesday, I talk to Ms. Cherry. I tell her how Gillicut goes on the rampage.

She says, "I'll mention it to the lunch aides."

I tell her they already know.

She says, "I'll talk to his teacher"—Mr. Hwang down the hall. And, "Let me know if it happens again, 'kay?"

Okay.

And then it does happen again. And again.

Friday, I go to see Ms. Cherry during recess when she has more time to listen. I explain how Gillicut's a bully and a dirtbug and a caveperson.

Ms. Cherry is sitting at her desk, eating a wrap sandwich. A bit of mayo blobs on her upper lip. I think that's why teachers don't like to eat in front of us kids. In case they look silly.

"Mr. Hwang already talked to Bruno and to Bruno's dad," says Ms. Cherry. "He said absolutely: no more kicking and no more taking lunch items from other kids. Bruno agreed."

"But he took my lunch *today*!" I protest.

"He did?"

"Yes!"

"Well, I'll tell Mr. Hwang. But let me share something with you, Hank." Ms. Cherry pats her complicated hair.

"What?"

"Mr. Hwang thinks Bruno could use some friends. Since the summer, his parents don't live together anymore. He's just with his dad, and he's been going through a rough time. He needs everyone to be nice to him."

No.

"Maybe if you offer to share your sprinkles, he'll offer to share something back. You could reach out!"

No, no.

"You can switch the situation around. You can be an ambassador of goodwill."

No, no, *no*.

"Remember, Hank," says Ms. Cherry. "Strangers are friends waiting to happen. We don't use words like *bully* and *dirtbug* and *caveperson* to talk about our friends, now, do we?"

And then, answering herself: "No. We don't. If you are using words like that with Bruno, the way you just did talking to me—well, then you're giving *him* a hard time, aren't you?"

"How did it go with Ms. Cherry?" Inkling asks later as we move our pieces around the Monopoly board. He's eating kidney beans with whipped cream on top, his new favorite dinner.

"Bleh," I say.

"What happened?"

I am too tired to tell the whole story. "Ms. Cherry understands Everyday Math," I tell Inkling. "But she does not understand people."

"I don't understand people, either," says Inkling, collecting the money on Free Parking. "Not liking squash, wanting to be alone in the bathroom, all that stuff is incomprehensible."

You understand us when it matters, I think.

But that's too mushy to say out loud.

Instead, I buy Park Place and build four houses.

Terror in the Aisles
of Health Goddess

On the weekend, Mom goes to Health Goddess, the natural-food store near our home. It's run by friends of my parents.

"Come on," I tell Inkling. "I'm gonna get you a squash now." He climbs onto my back, warm and heavy, and we go with Mom. I stroll through aisles of bean soup, almond butter, and other foods I don't like until we get to the produce section.

As we round the corner, Inkling's legs kick with excitement. He breathes hard in my ear.

And then I see it, too.

Squash! Piles and piles of squash! Tan ones, green ones, yellow. Even striped.

I read the signs: butternut, acorn squash, banana squash, and delicata.

"Mom!" I call. She is looking over the apples, selecting ones without bruises. "Can we get some squash?"

She crinkles her nose at me. "Hmm. What do you need it for?"

"Just to eat," I say, innocently. "I feel like squash. You know, um, for dinner."

"Hank, you know you don't like squash. When we had it at Aunt Sophia's, you made gagging noises."

"Tastes change. Maybe I like it now."

"That was only two months ago."

"Maybe I like it cooked a different way!"

"It was baked with brown sugar and butter."

Inkling whispers in my ear. "Bandapats eat it raw."

"You don't have to cook it," I tell Mom.

"You can't eat raw squash," she says. "Nobody eats raw squash, except maybe zucchini. Is that what you want, Hank? Zucchini?"

Inkling speaks fiercely in my ear: "No! No zucchini!"

"No!" I tell Mom. "I want—"

"Butternut," Inkling whispers.

"Butternut!"

Mom narrows her eyes at me. "You want to eat raw butternut squash for dinner."

"Yes!" I cry. "Please?"

"No." She selects a bunch of apples and puts them in a bag. "That's ridiculous, Hank. It's not even edible raw. I know you won't like it, and I don't want to waste money. Let's buy broccoli." She turns decisively and walks to the other end of the produce section, where she begins filling bags with green vegetables.

Inkling is panting on my back, muttering: "Squash here, squash there, squash piled high. But squash for Inkling? No squash for Inkling."

"Calm down," I say, under my breath. "I'll come shopping another day with Dad. Maybe I can get *him* to buy some."

"Want the squash. Need it now. Squash! Squash!"

"Keep your voice down!" I hiss.

Inkling begins muttering again—more to himself than to me. "Butternut. Acorn. Butternut. Acorn . . . Butternut!"

Suddenly, Inkling is not on my back anymore.

Where is he?

Oh.

Oh no.

There is a butternut squash with two bites out of it scootching down the aisle of Health Goddess.

As if it hopes no one will notice it.

Mom runs over from the broccoli and grabs my arm. "Hank, don't freak out," she says, "but I think there's a rat in here. See that squash moving across the floor?"

"Oh, I'm sure it's not a rat," I say, but I can't think of another reason the squash would be moving.

"Well, if it's not a rat, it's some other vermin. We can't have that here in Health Goddess." She runs to a corner of the market and grabs a broom. "Shoo!" she cries, chasing the squash.

Whack! She hits it hard, once.

The squash stops moving.

The squash wiggles, feebly, as if injured. Is Inkling okay?

Whack! Mom hits it again.

"Mom, stop!"

Erik, the guy who owns Health Goddess, runs over

to see what's up. "There's a rat under that squash," Mom tells him. "You can't see it, but it's there. Get another broom!"

Several customers are gathering round. Two are shrieking and standing on wooden produce boxes. One dad has scooped up his three-year-old, clutching the kid like there's a lion loose in the market.

The squash is trying to move across the floor again, heading toward the door.

Whack! Mom hits it again.

"Stop!" I cry.

And *slam!* Erik comes back with a mop and hits it from the other side. "Did you see it?" he yells. "I can't see it!"

Whack! Mom again.

"Don't hurt him!" I yell. But no one is listening to me. People are shrieking "Rat! Rat!" and "Get it out of here!" and things like that.

Slam! Erik lands a good one on the top of the butternut. Half of it breaks off.

Then the other half begins limping down the aisle—if squash can limp—and Mom runs after it. "Shoo! Out you go!"

I run after her and try to grab her arm, but she's fast, and she hits it again with her broom. *Whack!*

The half squash shatters into many, many pieces.

Mom looks down. No rat in sight. "Did it run outside? Hank, did you see it?"

I ignore her and drop to my knees, feeling around on the floor for Inkling.

He must be hurt. He might even be bleeding or have a broken bone.

"Maybe it was just a baby rat. Maybe it was a lost chipmunk," Mom is saying.

I touch the floor, the shelves, the corners, feeling around like a blind person.

"Hank, what are you doing?"

"Cleaning up the squash," I say, pushing some blobs of butternut around on the floor.

"Oh." Her face breaks into a smile. "That's nice. Since when are you such a helpful kid?"

She turns and begins talking to Erik about how the baby rat or chipmunk is probably still somewhere in the market, and it's really fast. That's why neither of them got a good look at it. They need to put out no-kill peanut-butter traps.

I go back to running my hands along the floors, searching for Inkling. He must be wounded, or he'd come to me. And he must be scared to make any noise, because now Erik's on the lookout for a rat.

My hand finally hits quivering fur and I can feel Inkling, shaking and limp, squeezed between two bins of granola. I'm so relieved I want to cry, but instead I pick him up. He crawls slowly onto my back, moving as if he's bruised all over.

Keeping him gently in place with one hand, I pick up the unshattered half of the butternut squash that's lying in the produce section. "Excuse me, Erik?" I say, interrupting his chat with Mom. "Since you probably can't sell this, would it be okay if I took it home?"

He tells me yes, and Inkling and I head outside and wait on a bench for Mom to finish her shopping.

"Yummy, yummy squashy goodness," Inkling mumbles to himself, as the butternut disappears in small, eager bites. He makes grunting noises as he eats.

In minutes, the whole thing is gone. Inkling burps in satisfaction.

When she comes outside, Mom asks me what happened to that squash I asked Erik for.

"I took a bite and you were right," I tell her. "I don't like it after all. I threw it in the trash. I don't know what I was thinking."

"I knew you wouldn't like it." She laughs. "I guess you learned a lesson, huh?"

"Yeah," I lie. "I did."

Invisible Blood

Inkling is bruised and shaken. He's got a cut on his back left leg, and he demands that I put ointment and a Band-Aid on it when we get home. I get the stuff and bring it to my bedroom.

"Where's your leg?" I ask, kneeling by the bottom bunk where he's lying on my pillow.

"Here."

"Where here?"

"Here!" His rough foot hits me gently in the nose.

"Okay, already." I take his leg in my hands and feel the ankle beneath the thick, damp fur. "I can't see any blood." I look down. My fingers feel wet, but they look as clean as ever.

"Where your left hand is touching," snaps Inkling. "It's a gaping wound, practically. I'm sure you're getting germs in it right now."

"Sorry."

"Did you wash your hands before you started this operation?"

I yank my hands away and open the tube of antibiotic cream. "Put your cut underneath the tube," I say. "That might work better."

I manage to squeeze the cream on and wrap a large Band-Aid around the leg where Inkling says the wound is. The bandage disappears as it sticks to Inkling's fur.

That night, Inkling sleeps on my pillow instead of in the laundry basket. I pet his fluffy neck in the darkness.

I hate not knowing what he looks like.

How can you really *know* someone if you don't know how he looks?

I know Nadia by her green hair and big boots—not the whole Nadia, but an important part of her. I know Chin by her dimples and the jeans with the holes, Dad by his scraggle beard, Mom by her chapped ice-cream-store hands.

Inkling has been here a while now, and all I can tell you is what my fingers know:

He's about the size of Rootbeer, but fatter.

He has claws and a bushy tail.

His nose is cold and wet.

His teeth are sharp.

But is he brown? Or blue? White?

Does his face look shifty? Bossy? Clever?

Thoughtful, like Chin's?

Or enthusiastic, like Dad's?

I've asked him over and over, but he never really answers.

"I'm extremely cute," he tells me when I ask again, tonight. "What else do you need to know?"

"Cute people don't like to be invisible," I point out. "Funny-looking people like to be invisible."

"I'm *naturally* invisible," says Inkling. "It's not like I could let you see me even if I wanted you to."

"Really?"

"Really."

"Not even for a few minutes?"

Inkling avoids the question. "Invisible is better for

me anyway. It's a rough world in this big city. Bandapats are endangered. I have to keep myself alive. If anyone got a glimpse—if anyone besides you knew about me—I'd end up in a science lab. Or even worse, a zoo."

"So you *can* be visible, sometimes?"

"No."

"You just said, 'If anyone got a glimpse.'"

"No, I didn't."

"Yes, you did."

"Wolowitz. Will you leave it alone? I'm an invisible bandapat."

We've had this conversation, or one very like it, lots of times.

But I can never leave it alone.

I want to see him so badly.

On Wednesdays, Chin and I have Theater of the Mind after school. It's where you stay late with the drama teacher and do projects. I like it because the drama teacher never complains about my overbusy imagination. He actually *likes* my overbusy imagination.

I go because Dad can't pick me up until the after-school rush is over at Big Round Pumpkin, and on

Wednesdays Nadia has PSAT study all afternoon. When he's off work, Dad picks up Chin, too. He arranged it with her mom at the start of the school year. I heard him on the phone saying stuff about "fostering their friendship" and how Hank "seems lonely since Alexander moved away."

I'd be annoyed, except Chin is fun to hang around with. Our Great Wall of China in matchsticks is nearly done, and she's already sent away for instructions on how to do a Taj Mahal. On Theater of the Mind days, we usually play alien schoolchildren in the park across the street, and then Dad takes us for Thai food. In alien schoolchildren, which I invented, Chin is a mean teacher and I am a variety of weirdo aliens she has to teach. The aliens all have cool powers they use to make trouble for the mean teacher. Superlong tentacles shoot out of their bodies and grab the chalk out of her hands; or brain control makes her think she is shrinking to the size of an ant when really she is normal.

Today, Chin and I race to climb this really big rock at one end of the park, because that's the best place to play alien schoolchildren. Dad heads over to chat with

some other parents in the far corner where the picnic tables are.

Chin gets on the rock right away, but my backpack is really heavy, so I bend over to put it down by a tree— and a foot hits me in the backside.

It's Gillicut.

Of course it's Gillicut.

It's not enough that I gave him half my lunch today;

he has to come torture me in the park, too.

My dad still hasn't come up with anything I can do to stop him. And Inkling hasn't, either.

"Leave me alone!" I say, turning.

"Make me," he growls.

Oh.

Um.

I have no idea how to make him.

Also, he's not doing anything right this minute. So I can't figure out how I'd even make him when nothing's happening.

"You can't just go kicking people, Bruno," says Chin from high on the rock.

"Why not?"

"Because . . . you can't," she says lamely.

"But I just did. So, yeah. I can."

"Why are you always picking on Hank?" Chin demands.

I am standing there. Like an idiot. Like a victim. Saying nothing.

"He annoys me," says Gillicut. "Plus, he stinks at soccer. And he has sprinkies in his lunch."

"What if he *stops bringing* sprinkles?" Chin asks.

Gillicut grabs the sleeves of my sweatshirt, tugs them down over my hands, and shakes them up and down, hard. "Oh, he doesn't want to do *that*!" he says, jumping as he shakes me. "Don't stop bringing sprinkies, Spanky! You wouldn't like to see what happens when I don't get my sprinkies!"

He releases me, laughing.

I am breathing hard.

I want to kick him.

I *could* kick him, from where I'm standing. He's doubled over, laughing.

I should kick him.

I should.

Maybe then he'd leave me alone.

But—

I can't quite make my foot kick out.

It's like, *I* want to do it, but my foot is too scared.

I may not be a pacifist exactly—because I'm not sure you can call yourself a pacifist when you've built a Great Wall of China from matchsticks plus a set of airplane bombers from Legos—but let's be honest: I have zero fighting skills.

"Is the Spanky Baby gonna cry now?" Gillicut asks.

"Does it want its spanky mommy?"

"Why are you such a dirtbug?" I spit out.

"Oh, am I? Ask your spanky mommy why."

"His dad is here, actually," Chin mutters from the rock.

"Go on, Baby," says Gillicut. "Run away like you always do and ask your spanky mommy."

Oh, I hate him so much.

So much, so much.

"Just 'cause *your* mom doesn't want you anymore doesn't mean you get to call *me* a baby," I snarl.

It's a mean thing to say, but words are all I've got.

He reels back like I've hit him. "Don't say that. Shut up about my mom!"

Oh no.

I've really done it now.

Gillicut's mom moved out, Ms. Cherry said.

Who knew I could be so mean? And so stupid?

Gillicut's hand balls into a fist.

I'm not sure whether to run or duck—or just stand there and take whatever he's going to dish out.

But then, there is Dad, peeking over the big rock. "Hank! Sasha!" he says. "You guys ready for dumplings?"

I want to run and tell Dad everything that just happened.

I want to tell him and have him take my side: stride over to Gillicut and make sure that dirtbug never bothers me again. I want Dad to wrap his arms around me and tell me I'm all right and Gillicut is all wrong.

But—I've just said that thing. That awful, awful thing about Gillicut's mom not wanting him.

When I think about explaining *that* to Dad, my face feels hot and I want to crawl under the big rock.

I can't bear to have my father look at me with disappointment in his eyes.

I don't ever want him to know I've been so mean.

Sasha jumps down from the rock and runs over to

Dad. "Let's get out of here," she says.

Dad does a silly little dumpling dance. "Dumplings, yumplings, roly-poly dumplings! Eat you, eat you, we will eat you UP!"

Chin laughs.

Dad laughs.

Gillicut speaks under his breath. "You're gonna pay for what you just said," he tells me.

I know it.

I know I'm gonna pay.

Dad and Sasha are walking out of the park. I shoulder my backpack and follow them without a word.

A New Plan

We are half a block from Rice, the Thai restaurant we always go to. I am trailing behind.

Thinking about Gillicut and what he's going to do to me next day at school.

About how I could say such a cruel thing. How it just popped out of my mouth, one of the meanest things a person can say to another person.

About Chin, and how she stood up for me.

I am inside my head, hardly noticing my feet on the sidewalk or the cars going by, when: "Wolowitz! Let me out!"

A voice is right in my ear.

What?

"It's hot in here!"

Inkling is hiding in my backpack.

He's never been in my backpack before.

How did he get in there?

When did he get in there?

I unzip it. There's a thud, and then a *pitter-pat*, and I know he's walking along beside me.

"I came during Theater of the Mind," says Inkling, in explanation. "I wanted to see that Gillicut for myself. Plus, there was nothing good on television."

Ahead of us, Dad and Chin open the door to the restaurant. "We're going in, okay, Hank?" Dad calls. "Come inside."

I wave to say I'll catch up to them.

"How did you find me?" I ask Inkling. He has always refused to come to school before. Too scared of crowds.

"I made my way to Big Round Pumpkin from the heights of the Himalayan mountains. I think I can find your elementary school that's three blocks away from your apartment."

Oh.

"Anyway," says Inkling. "Gillicut is a dirtbug and a caveperson."

I sigh. "Yeah."

"I saw what happened in the park."

I nod.

"You were right. He hates you. And he's really big and mean, and now that you said his mommy doesn't want him, he hates you even more."

Yeah, I know.

"So." Inkling pauses dramatically.

"So what already?"

"So despite the fact that I'm seriously squash-deprived, I see the urgency of your problem. I've got a new plan."

Dad pops his head out of Rice. "Hank! You can't just stand around on the street. Come in and look at the menu."

I have to go in without finishing the conversation. We order crispy spring rolls and vegetable dumplings and fried tofu. I feed Inkling under the table.

"You're hogging the dumplings, Hank," complains Chin.

I can't explain that Inkling has been poking my leg

really hard and even grabbing dumplings off my plate. I try and feed him the rest of my tofu, but he just pops up and snags the last dumpling when Chin is in the bathroom and Dad is talking to the waiter.

After dinner we all play Boggle for a bit in Chin's apartment; then Dad and I head home. I have to shower and brush my teeth and get into bed. I don't have time to talk to Inkling until late.

Now we sit by the window, looking down at the streetlamps and the lights from the shops that are still open at night.

"What's your new plan?" I ask.

Inkling pauses for dramatic effect. "You've got to pounce."

"What?"

"Climb up in a really big tree and wait until Gillicut comes by. Then—*kah-blam!* You drop right on top of him, and you take *his* sprinkles! Like me when I nabbed that pumpkin off that kangaroo."

"Gillicut doesn't *have* any sprinkles," I say. "That's why he takes mine."

"Take his whole lunch box then."

"He buys lunch."

Inkling thinks. "I know. Wait for pizza Friday, then get in the tree and *kah-blam!* Take his pizza!" He lowers his voice, coaxing. "And if you don't want to eat it yourself, you can always give it to me. You know I like pizza, Wolowitz."

"There are no trees in the lunchroom," I tell Inkling.

"What?"

"It's indoors. There aren't any trees."

"Oh. Yeah. So what are you going to drop from?"

"I'm not dropping."

"Are there pipes in the ceiling?" Inkling asks. "Could you drop from a pipe?"

"Yes, there are pipes. But no, I could not."

Inkling sits in silence for a moment. "*I* could," he says at last. "A pipe's not that different from a branch, and I've dropped from more branches than you can count."

"Maybe I should apologize for what I said about his mom," I say. "And keep bringing him sprinkles like he wants. Maybe then I'll live through the school year."

"Are you kidding?" Inkling cries. "No! This Gillicut needs to be dropped on. When he's done with you, he's gonna start taking sprinkles from the first graders. Then the kindergartners. Then the bitty preschoolers. We have to stop him before he goes on a preschooler rampage."

He could be right.

"I'm coming to school with you, pizza Friday," Inkling announces. "Got that?"

"You hate crowds. You're squash deprived."

"True. But I like pizza. Anyhow, I gotta risk it. It's the only way I can pay the Hetsnickle. Friday at noon, right? I'll be there on the pipe."

I nod.

A thing about Inkling is, he doesn't take no for an answer.

Land o' Pumpkins

On Inkling's advice, I survive Thursday by playing sick. We can't ambush Gillicut till Friday, and I have to stay alive for that to happen, so I'd better just not go to school. I tell Mom at the breakfast table: "I think I got bit by a rare South American beetle, one of those ones with venom that gives you a fainting sickness and makes your legs swell up all weird and red."

"Oh, really?" She feels my forehead and takes a thoughtful bite of granola.

"My legs are really itchy. I don't think I should go to school."

"Dad said something about a boy who was mean to you in the park yesterday," Mom says, bending down to examine my completely normal-looking legs. "Was that the boy you talked about before? Is he still giving you trouble?"

I nod. I hadn't realized Dad even noticed Gillicut in the park. He didn't say anything. He never did come up with any advice for me.

"Does that boy have anything to do with your South American beetle illness?" Mom asks.

"No," I say. "There was this strange beetle yesterday that climbed on me and probably bit me."

She pats my shoulder. "Sounds like a twenty-four-hour sickness. Right?"

"I think so."

"Okay. You can stay home. But what will you do all morning? I can be here, but I have a ton of bills to pay for the shop." Suddenly I notice that my mom has lines around her mouth. Her hair is showing gray because she hasn't gone to the salon like she usually does.

"I'll play with my imaginary friend," I tell her. "No problem."

She laughs.

* * *

Inkling cheats at Monopoly. But I beat him at Blokus.

"Wolowitz," he tells me as he's reading the strategy tips. "I have news."

"You do?"

"Squash news."

"Did you find some?"

"Not exactly."

"Did you figure out how to get some?"

"Kind of."

"'Cause it would be good for you to have some squash before tomorrow," I say. "So your strength is up for the big attack."

"Yeah, well. Squash in Brooklyn. I'll believe that when I see it."

"I thought you said—"

"Wolowitz," interrupts Inkling. "I hate to tell you this, but after I save your life tomorrow, I gotta go."

"What do you mean?"

He heaves a sigh. "The squash problem. It's killing me. I told you I couldn't stay here without squash."

"For serious?"

"There's a pumpkin farm in upstate New York. Land

o' Pumpkins. I read about it in the paper."

"Oh." I am in shock.

I feel dizzy.

Inkling is moving away.

Forever.

And not even against his will.

"Did you know there's a holiday called Halloween?" Inkling asks.

I nod.

"And on Halloween, human beings actually hollow out pumpkins and *throw away* all the yummy inside bits?" Inkling asks.

"I've heard of that, yeah." My voice comes out choked.

"Wolowitz, I gotta get to this Land o' Pumpkins. I'm one of the last bandapats. If I don't eat squash regularly, I'm gonna . . . You know I've only had that half a butternut since I got to Brooklyn."

"I tried to get you squash. I really did."

"I know. But it's a serious situation. A pumpkin farm is a much better place for a bandapat than a squashless Brooklyn full of rootbeers."

"Don't go," I whisper.

"You'll get over it," Inkling says. "This is not a

life-or-death problem for you."

"Please, Inkling. I'll try even harder."

"Wolowitz, you've tried and you've tried. You're just not a guy with a lot of squash. It's a fact you've got to accept about yourself."

"I'm so, so sorry," I say.

"I'm sorry, too," he says. "But once I've paid the Hetsnickle, I'm off to Land o' Pumpkins. It's just the way it's got to be."

I excuse myself and go to the kitchen. I open the freezer and pull out a tub of Heath bar brownie ice cream. It's not even my favorite flavor, but I eat two bowls of it anyway before Mom comes in and makes me stop.

At noon Mom has to go to Big Round Pumpkin. Inkling and I tag along with her. I pretend to be sick in the overlook.

I lie on the floor up there in a fog. Inkling and I don't talk. I wouldn't even know he was there with me if it wasn't for an occasional cough from his favorite corner.

I read a book about volcanoes I got from the library.

I do my math homework.

I start drawing a picture of me and Inkling—only

there's nothing to draw when I get to him. I don't know what he looks like.

I crumple the picture and toss it into the recycling.

After school, Nadia comes by to walk me home, but we go over past our building to Smith Street first because she wants to look in the window of this store that sells funny hats.

She's talking about how she wants to buy one for her boyfriend, Max, but can't decide between the one that looks like a Mohawk and the one that has skulls on it. I'm about to tell her that the one with stegosaurus spikes is much better and it's three dollars cheaper than either of the ones she's thinking about—when I see the face of an animal, down by my knee, reflected in the window.

It disappears almost as soon as I see it—takes off down the block, and I've caught nothing but a flash of black eyes and a puff of orangey fur—but I'm sure it's Inkling. "I'm running home!" I shout to Nadia, and zoom around the corner and to the end of the block where our apartment building is.

As I get to our steps, I can hear Inkling wheezing from the run. Nadia is still at the other end of the street, moving slow, weighed down by schoolbooks.

"I just saw you in the store window," I gasp.

"No, you didn't."

"Yes, I did."

"You saw a rootbeer."

"No."

"Then you saw a squirrel."

"No squirrel is that big."

"You saw nothing, Wolowitz. Stop imagining."

"I saw *you*!" I say. "But barely. Won't you let me see you some more?"

"Never."

"Inkling!" I say. "Please? Now that I know I can actually see you, I can hardly stand it."

"I can't take the chance, Wolowitz. Bandapats are nearly extinct. If they put me in a lab or a zoo surrounded by mirrors, I don't think I can take it, that's all. I can't live that way."

"Pretty please?" I beg.

"No, no, no," says Inkling. "This conversation is over."

I Play a Mean Trick

My parents both work until eight o'clock tonight, so Nadia's in charge of dinner. She steams broccoli and makes us a package of organic macaroni and cheese. Then she plugs her headphones into the computer and does her homework.

I decide to get a proper look at Inkling, whether he wants me to or not.

Because he's leaving me for a pumpkin patch upstate.

Because if I can see him, I'll have something concrete to remember when he's gone.

I'm not sure where he is in the apartment, but I put

some Oatie Puffs in a small bowl. I tuck that and my most special pop-up book under my arm. "I'm going to the bathroom to have a snack of delicious Oatie Puffs and to read about helicopters," I say loudly. "And I'm leaving the door open, because I don't need privacy right now!"

"Don't touch my volumizer putty," Nadia says, taking off her headphones. "Or my scrunchy gel."

"I would never," I say. And it's *sort of* true: Since I fluffed my hair at school three weeks ago, I have zero interest in hair products.

"Well, someone messed with it yesterday."

Inkling. He's been volumizing his fluff!

"Maybe Mom borrowed some," I say. "Did I mention I'll be reading my helicopter pop-up book out loud? And that there will be Oatie Puffs?"

"Why are you bringing *cereal* to the bathroom?" asks Nadia. "That's kind of disgusting."

"I like the light in there," I say. "The tiles are cool on a hot day."

"You have a weird brain," says Nadia. "I'm telling you, Hank."

"I'm taking these *super yummy* Oatie Puffs to

the bathroom now," I yell.

"Good-*bye* already," says Nadia, putting her headphones back on.

I get settled in the bathroom. I don't touch Nadia's hair stuff, but just to tease her I put the eyeliners in the cup where the toothbrushes live. I'm only in there for a minute or two when I see the door swing.

Ha ha!

I pounce. Fur and muscle flail in my hands.

Ha ha again!

"Let go, you crazy human!" Inkling barks, wiggling madly.

I keep holding on. "I'm just going to look at you!"

"Put me down!" He twists and flails. "You're insulting my dignity!"

Ignoring his struggles, I put one hand under Inkling's backside, and with the other I grab the scruff of his thick neck. He's kicking hard with his back feet, snorting. I know he has a right to be mad—but I can't stand it anymore.

I need to know what he looks like.

I need to know his face, the way I know the faces of my family. I need it now, before he leaves me for Land o' Pumpkins. I need it—*today*—because yesterday I was meaner than I've ever been to anyone; and 'cause tomorrow, Gillicut may kill me.

Keeping tight hold of Inkling's wiggling body, I climb onto a chair I've pushed in front of our medicine cabinet.

"My teeth are by your neck, Wolowitz!" cries Inkling. "I can bite your neck if I want to! Bandapats have serious teeth!"

"Be quiet," I whisper. "You don't want Nadia coming in here."

"My serious teeth are right by your neck!"

But I know he won't hurt me.

He would never hurt me. I trust Inkling completely, which is why I need to see him so badly. I lift his squirming body and: There we are, in the mirror.

Me, just how I always look.

Inkling, twitching and snapping.

He's reddish orange with black stripes around the neck. Big black eyes. Creamy white ears. Stripy rings down his fat tail.

His face isn't shifty or clever or content. It's . . . friendly. Even though he's struggling in my arms.

"Hank!" The door opens all the way, and Nadia is standing there.

I drop Inkling.

He scrabbles as he falls and grabs the back of the wooden chair.

It tips.

I tip.

We all three tip backward and—

Bam!

The chair hits the Oatie Puffs bowl,

the cereal sprays across the room,

I land in the tub,

Inkling's underneath me,

my head hits the tile,

Nadia shrieks,

the room spins,

Oatie Puffs rain down on us—

and I am lying in pain in the tub, staring up at the shower head and feeling Inkling worm himself from under my legs. He heaves out and then I hear the soft click of claws going across the bathroom tile.

"Are you okay?" Nadia pulls me to a sitting position.

Everything aches.

Nadia inspects my head where I hit it. She strokes my hair. "I don't think you're bleeding. Does it hurt? Are you going to cry? Poor Hank." She puts her mouth on my head but doesn't exactly kiss.

"I'm okay," I say, squirming. "I'm fine."

"Then why were you standing on a chair?" She sounds mad now. "Why were you yelling at the mirror?"

"I—"

"And why, why, *why* were you eating Oatie Puffs in the bathroom? Why can't you just watch TV like a normal person?" Nadia rakes her hand through her green hair. "Why, Hank, why?"

"Because I'm *not* a normal person!" I scream. "I'm not. Why can't you just *like* that about me?"

Nadia doesn't answer. I climb out of the tub and stomp off to my room.

Inkling sulks in the laundry basket the rest of the evening. After my parents come home and Mom tucks me into bed, I try to make up with him.

I crawl into my closet so we can talk. "You're cute,

you know." I start with flattery.

"What, you're surprised?" Inkling barks. "Of course I'm cute."

"I knew you were furry," I say, "and very soft and nicely fluffy, but—"

"Just stop there. Don't be insulting."

"I thought—"

"All bandapats are cute, and I am one especially cute bandapat. I've told you before. There should be no surprise." I can hear him adjust his position in the basket.

"Fine," I say. "I meant it as a compliment."

"I woulda been cuter if you hadn't been holding me by the scruff," complains Inkling. "I have a nice fluff of fur around my neck area. You couldn't see it."

"Will you let me pick you up again?" I coax. "Let me hold you up to the mirror so I can get a better look at your cuteness?"

"In your dreams," says Inkling.

He's still mad.

"I'm sorry I grabbed you," I say. "I'm sorry we fell down."

"I'm *invisible*, Wolowitz," snaps Inkling. "That means I'm *not visible*, and *not visible* means you can't see me.

Not visible is how I like it to be and how bandapats have survived through the ages until we got endangered. Really, just what part of this did you not understand when you lured me into the bathroom with cereal and pop-up books—just so you could jump me?"

"I tried to be gentle," I protest.

"Oh!" Inkling's voice is cross. "Thanks for being gentle when you were sneak-attacking me. Thanks for being gentle while you bullied me just like Gillicut bullies you. Thanks for being gentle while you manhandle me like I'm a stupid pet."

"I *am* sorry," I say. "It seems so strange to spend all this time together and not know what you look like. Especially when you're leaving."

"You're asking to look at me again, Wolowitz."

"Yes, but—"

"When I just said I like to be invisible! That doesn't sound like sorry to me."

"I am too sorry."

"Maybe I should leave first thing tomorrow," says Inkling. "Maybe I don't owe you a Hetsnickle debt of honor anymore after all."

"Fine," I say. "I never asked you to owe me anything."

"Fine, then. Now can you leave me alone? I'm extremely tired from being manhandled."

"Fine."

"Yes, fine."

"Fine yourself," I say.

I get back in bed.

I can't sleep.

And I can't sleep.

I lie there, thinking, *I have an invisible friend, and he won't accept my apology.*

I have an invisible friend, and he won't talk to me.

I have an invisible friend, but he doesn't even like me anymore.

I am a dirtbug and a caveperson, that's why.

Rampage

Friday. Pizza day.

When I get up, Inkling's not in the laundry basket, not in the back of the closet, not on my pillow.

Nowhere.

Maybe he's gone for good.

I should have understood about him not wanting to be visible.

I shouldn't have grabbed him.

Shouldn't have.

Shouldn't have.

Shouldn't have.

"Inkling!" I call. "Inkling, where are you?"

But there is no answer. No matter how many times I call.

The lunchroom is always loud on pizza day. More people buy their lunch than usual, and even some of the teachers stand on line.

"Gillicut's going to rampage," says Chin.

"What else is new?"

"I mean, he's going to rampage extra. After what you said about his mom."

"I know." My stomach drops.

I have no plan. I have no protection. I have no Inkling.

I will be facing this rampaging Gillicut alone, which is probably what I deserve after all I've done—but it stinks anyway.

We pour into the lunchroom. Most of the kids follow Ms. Cherry into the pizza line, except Chin and I have box lunch. Chin because she only likes apple-butter-and-pickle sandwiches, and me because my parents won't let me buy. We grab a table behind a large post in the center of the room, hoping Gillicut won't see us.

No luck.

I've just unpacked my food and am biting into my apple when suddenly he is standing next to me, unloading his tray.

What? Why unload?

He's never unloaded before.

Is he going to sit down with us?

Why would he sit down with us?

He does sit down. Makes himself at home. Like he's welcome to eat lunch with us or something.

"Hey, Spank." Gillicut waves his hand in front of my face. "Didn't I tell you not to start eating until we've had our daily chat?"

I look up.

Not a lunch aide in sight.

"Sprinkie tax," Gillicut says, reaching over to grab my Tupperware.

I hold my breath.

"I'll take these, too," he says, reaching for a bag of Cheddar Bunnies.

Gillicut dumps the bunnies on the table and shoves some in his mouth.

What's he going to do next?

He must have some evil plan or he wouldn't have sat down.

Chin has her arms protectively around her apple-butter-and-pickle sandwich.

"May I sit here?" Ms. Cherry stands over us, holding a tray of pizza, cranberry juice, and fruit salad.

I breathe out.

If a teacher is going to sit with us, I should be safe. What can Gillicut do with Ms. Cherry sitting across from him?

"Sure," I answer. Chin scoots over to make room.

"I've decided I should eat with my students on pizza day," says Ms. Cherry, setting her food down and touching her complicated hair. She eases herself onto the bench. "I never get a chance to just chat with you guys!" She reaches over and pats my hand. "I love to connect with kids outside of the classroom."

"Hello, Ms. Cherry," says Gillicut, chewing my bunnies.

"Bruno, did Hank give you his ice-cream-shop sprinkles today?" she says, noticing the container.

I'm about to say "No!" when Gillicut kicks me under the table. "Thank you so much for the sprinkies, Hank!" He smiles. "Ms. Cherry, would you like some? They're rainbow."

"Hank!" Ms. Cherry pats my hand again. "Did you decide to be an ambassador of goodwill? Because I think you *did*!"

"Not really," I say. "I—"

"I love sprinkles," says Ms. Cherry, picking up the Tupperware and peeking in. "My favorite ice-cream combo is peppermint with chocolate. Oh, and whipped cream. What about you, Sasha?"

But before Chin can answer, Ms. Cherry drops the container and screams.

All Tomato Sauce and Anger

Ms. Cherry bends over, yelling. She clutches her hair, which is rapidly unwinding, as if by magic. Her lunch tray skids across the table, spraying cranberry juice everywhere. She falls to the floor, yowling and thrashing as if some invisible—

Oh.

It's Inkling.

He is here, after all!

Despite what I did to him, he didn't leave me to face Gillicut alone.

Only: He has dropped on the wrong person. He

dropped on Ms. Cherry!

The items on the tabletop skid to the ground as Inkling launches himself at Gillicut's pizza. He must grab the crust in his mouth because the slice lifts into the air, waving violently so that the triangle part flaps.

Whomp! It hits Gillicut hard across the face, smearing him with cheese and pepperoni.

And *whomp!* Back the other way with the crust side.

Gillicut is all over tomato sauce and anger. He tackles me and rolls me on the floor. I can see Ms. Cherry flailing, trying to pull herself to standing, high heels slipping on a puddle of cranberry juice. Gillicut and I land several feet from her, rolling onto the plastic carton of blueberry yogurt from my lunch. I can feel it burst under my head. Gillicut's hot face is right in mine. He's crushing me, and I can barely breathe. The yogurt is all in my hair. Chin yanks at Gillicut's shirt, trying to get him off me, but he bats her away.

Where is Inkling?

Why isn't he helping?

Oh, wait—I bet he stopped to eat Gillicut's pizza.

Yep.

Inkling is filling himself with cheesy goodness while Gillicut is rampaging on me! I kick and flail.

"Do you want me to teach you a lesson?" Gillicut asks.

"What a stupid question," I squeak. "Like you could teach me anything."

"I told you I'd make you pay."

I don't answer, twisting my body to try to get out from under.

Gillicut's fingers pinch my neck and twist, hard—

Oh.

Ms. Cherry is standing over us.

Gillicut drops his hand.

"Boys!" says Ms. Cherry, sharply. "Are you two *fighting*?"

"Yes!" cries Chin. "They are!"

"No, we're not!" Gillicut stands up, releasing me. "It was all a big accident. A misunderstanding. I'm so sorry I fell over on you, Hank!"

He eyes Ms. Cherry but talks to me. I am lying on the floor in shock, cranberry juice and yogurt in my hair, sore in several places.

"Let me help you get some napkins," says Gillicut,

fake and hearty. "You have yogurt on your hair, and I think I have pizza on my face. Ha ha! I have pizza on my face, don't I?" He laughs. Actually laughs, while smiling at Ms. Cherry.

I am staring at Gillicut's thick calves beneath his shorts. His bony ankles going into sneakers without socks.

His ankles.

Horrible, mean, bully ankles.

I want to bite him.

I really do.

Want to lunge my head forward and bite Gillicut's ankle as hard as I can, waggling my head around to make it hurt more, the way Inkling told me.

But just like the other day in the park—*I* want to do it, but my teeth are too scared.

"Ahhhhhh!" Gillicut goes down, anyway, hitting the floor with a thud and flailing his legs around, kicking in pain.

Inkling!

He's not too scared to bite. I can see his teeth marks in Gillicut's ankle—

"Ahhhhhh!" He's throwing his legs around to get Inkling off him.

I start to sit up but, ow! Gillicut kicks me in the head and I go down again. Gillicut and Inkling and I are all tangled up now. There's fur in my face and a foot against my shoulder—

"Hank! This is deeply inappropriate!"

Miss Cherry looms.

Reaches down.

Grabs.

Seconds later, I am standing. She has me firmly by the shoulder.

Gillicut is on the floor.

I'm dizzy. My head aches where he kicked me.

I'm not even sure what happened. I have no idea where Inkling is.

"We don't bite our friends, Hank!" Ms. Cherry scolds.

What?

Before I know it, she's marched me out of the lunch-room and we're heading down the hall to the principal's office while a student "buddy" takes Gillicut to the nurse.

"I didn't bite anyone," I say.

"Oh? How did Bruno get bitten, then?" Ms. Cherry says sarcastically. "Some invisible creature bit him?"

I know I can't explain Inkling to Ms. Cherry. But it doesn't matter, because she doesn't wait for an answer.

"I want you to remember our motto," she goes on. "Strangers are friends you haven't gotten to know yet."

"Gillicut isn't a stranger or a friend," I say. "He's my enemy. I told you what he does to me."

"You don't have enemies," Ms. Cherry snaps. "You have friends and future friends. That's what you have." Her blouse is stained, and her complicated hairdo is back up but lopsided.

I don't reply.

As I sit in the front office, waiting for the principal, I feel Inkling's warm body press against my leg. He's wheezing slightly, as if he's been running to catch up with me.

I reach down and pick him up as soon as Ms. Cherry departs to teach class.

"You fluffed up your fur real well," Inkling whispers, his mouth near my ear. "I bet that Gillicut was scared stupid."

Huh?

I reach up to feel my hair.

It's standing on end because of the yogurt.

"Thanks," I say. I kick my feet against the bench. "And thanks for saving my life today."

"Bandapat code of honor," Inkling says. "Glad to do it."

Little Dude, Don't Bite

I am suspended for the rest of the day and sent home from school directly.

My parents are really, really mad at me. I have never seen them this upset.

It is not pretty.

When they calm down, Dad sits me down in the grown-up bedroom for a private talk.

"Little dude." His eyes are sad and concerned. "Don't bite."

"But—"

"Don't bite. No matter what happens. Ever."

"I didn't bite him," I say.

"There were teeth marks," he says. "The school nurse found your teeth marks."

"They were—"

I give up and go silent. I can't explain.

Dad rubs his scraggle beard. "In this family, we are pacifists," he says finally. "There is always a peaceable solution, little dude. Always."

"Okay."

"That means no more biting, or you're in big trouble."

"Okay."

"I know he pinched you, and even knocked you down, but . . . It's like the laws of the outback took over that lunchroom or something. What you did was wrong."

I see how sad he looks, how disappointed in me he is.

I think, *He doesn't even know I said that awful, awful thing about Gillicut's mom.*

I hate knowing I'm the kind of person who'd hurt someone's feelings that way.

But I do know it.

And I can't erase it.

"I'm really sorry, Dad," I say.

* * *

Saturday afternoon, Inkling is at the library looking at maps of upstate New York so he can find Land o' Pumpkins. Chin comes to the ice-cream store with her mom. She gets strawberry and hot fudge in a dish, and joins me in the overlook.

She says Gillicut had his ankle washed out with rubbing alcohol. Rumor from the kid who was his "nurse buddy": He bawled like a baby. He got bandaged up and came back to class walking with a limp.

His father picked him up early.

I feel a twinge of remorse. It probably really hurt, if Gillicut was crying.

Chin says she tried to tell Ms. Cherry that Gillicut started it all, "but Ms. Cherry said that she was there, sitting at our table. She said she saw everything, thank you very much. Bruno fell over on Hank and apologized for the accident. He even offered to get napkins. Then, for no reason at all, Hank bit Bruno. End of story."

I sigh.

There is no arguing with Ms. Cherry.

"What would you say, Chin," I ask, "if I told you it wasn't me that bit Gillicut?"

"What?"

"It was my . . . um . . . invisible friend who bit him. And we planned the ambush. What would you say?"

Chin laughs. "I'd say, how dumb do you think I am?"

"Still, what if I told you I really did have an invisible friend?"

"I'd say you should have your eyes checked."

"For serious."

She eats a spoonful of ice cream. "I'd say, I'm not invisible."

Wow.

Chin has been hanging out with me for almost a year, but she's never called me her friend until now.

I feel pretty cheerful at that.

"Hey," she says. "Do you think your parents would let you walk with me to the corner store? I got my allowance today, and I really want a box of Altoids."

I swear, I will never understand girls. Who would want Altoids when they could buy Oreos or Gummi worms?

"Yeah," I say. "I bet they will."

Then an idea comes to me.

A good idea. An important idea. I don't know why I didn't think of it before.

An idea to maybe make Inkling stay. Even though he's paid his Hetsnickle debt.

"Wait five minutes, 'kay?" I tell Chin. "There's something I realized I gotta do."

I climb down the ladder and run to the cash register. Mom is working the counter, scooping cones and taking people's money. "I want a job," I tell her.

It's something I should have said a long time ago.

"You do?" She wipes her hands on her apron.

"I want to earn extra money so I can go to the store with Chin," I tell her. "And maybe pay off the Lego airport faster. And pay Nadia back for the pop-up book. Like, could I take out all the recycling for you? Bag it up? Bring it to the sidewalk for pickup?"

Mom looks down at me. Then at the full recycle bins.

"I shouldn't just be sitting around the overlook all the time," I say. "I'm in the fourth grade."

There is a line of customers.

Nadia is scooping and Dad is fixing a broken cooler. "Yes, actually," Mom says. "That would be a huge help. How does a dollar sound?"

"How about five, to do it every day this week?" I say.

"Sure."

"And maybe other days I could wipe counters? Or fill napkin holders? I want to earn some money of my own, regular."

Mom smiles. "Yes, Hank. We could use your help, actually."

I bag up the recycling from all three bins and lug it out. Then I spray the bins with air freshener and put in new bags. I even sweep up a napkin and two spoons on the floor so the recycle area looks really good when I'm done.

Mom gives me a five-dollar bill.

"Thanks for waiting," I say to Chin. "I needed money."

"Whatcha gonna get?"

"Squash," I answer. "They have squash at that corner fruit market, right?"

"I dunno."

"I'm pretty sure I saw acorn there, if not butternut."

"I swear," mutters Chin, shaking her head as we walk together down the block. "I will never understand boys."

Destroy This Postcard

Later that day I get a postcard from Wainscotting.

> Wolowitz!
> Everyone here calls me Alexander. They do
> not know that in reality I am a secret agent
> named Wainscotting.
> Do not tell them, okay?
> DESTROY THIS POSTCARD!
> Your friend forever,
> AW

Getting the card makes me miss Wainscotting. A lot.

But then I realize: I haven't been thinking about him that much. Not all the time. Not the way I used to.

I've been busy, I guess.

With Inkling. With Chin after school. With my family.

I write back, on one of Big Round Pumpkin's publicity postcards.

Alexander!
(I call you that to keep your secret.)
I thought I could not survive fourth grade without you.
And.
It.
Has not.
Been.
Pretty.
But: I am still here.
Friends forever,
HW

I walk to the mailbox with Inkling on my back. He

gobbled up the squash I bought him earlier, but my new cash flow didn't convince him to stay. He's still leaving for Land o' Pumpkins first thing Monday morning on the train. He wants to be there for Halloween. Apparently they have something called a Pumpkin-Carving Extravaganza, and he doesn't want to miss it.

"I guess there won't be any address where I can send you postcards," I say. "Will there?"

"Nah," says Inkling. "I don't think so."

"Can you send *me* a postcard?"

"Maybe one. To let you know I'm okay."

"That's it? Just one?"

"Stamps are hard to come by."

"I just—"

I don't know what to say. I know I can't ask Inkling to stay.

"Aw, Wolowitz," he says, patting my shoulder. "Don't get mushy on me, now."

But I do get mushy.

I mean, I cry a little.

"I wish you a great time," I finally tell him. "And a lot of really yummy pumpkins."

I Figured I'd Come for Lunch

Monday, I walk into the lunchroom alone. "Wolowitz! You want to sit with us?" Chin calls, as she heads off with the girls.

I shake my head. "Maybe tomorrow."

I don't want to sit with them because even though Locke, Linderman, and Daley are fairly nice, I don't know how today is going to be.

Is Gillicut going to come and demand his sprinkles, like before?

Or something worse?

Whatever he's going to do, I don't want him to do it

in front of those girls.

I pick an empty table in a corner and open my lunch box. My back is to the wall, so I can see Gillicut when he approaches. I take out my yogurt and begin to mix it to the perfect purple color.

Blueberry yogurt. Blueberry yogurt.

Is he coming over? I glance up, but I don't see him.

I will myself to stay calm.

Blueberry yogurt. Blueberry yogurt.

He's hurt you before, and you've survived, I think.

Blueberry yogurt. Blueberry yogurt.

I look up to see Gillicut—and he's walking with his tray to the other side of the lunchroom. Way far away from me. He sits down with a kid called Joo and opens his milk.

He sees me looking at him.

We lock eyes.

He looks down.

And then I realize:

Gillicut's not taking my sprinkles.

He is not coming over at all.

Not today, and not tomorrow.

Because Gillicut is scared of me now.

Scared.

Of me.

He thinks I bit him. And biting—it's scary. And kinda weird. Much more violent than the twist-pinching and kicking and stuff that he's been doing to me.

It doesn't matter that it wasn't really me.

He's afraid.

My shoulders relax. The room looks brighter.

The future shines.

As I take a bite of yogurt, I hear a thump and feel Inkling's furry body scrambling from the chair next to me onto the table.

"You're here!" I say. My face bursts into a grin. "I thought you went to Land o' Pumpkins. We said good-bye."

"Well, I figured I'd come for lunch," he answers.

"Did you miss your train upstate? Will you be able to get another?"

"I was on my way to the station," says Inkling, "and I got to thinking you might need my help with Gillicut today."

"You paid the Hetsnickle on pizza Friday," I say. "You know you don't owe me anymore."

"Nah. See, pizza Friday wasn't the Hetsnickle." Inkling snorts. "I realized that this morning. All I did was bite a nine-year-old on the ankle."

"So?"

"In the Mexican swamplands, where I come from, that would be nothing but a warm-up to a day of combat."

"But—"

"I still owe you, Wolowitz. Dropping on Gillicut was nothing compared to what *you* did for me when that rootbeer attacked," says Inkling. "Or when people mauled me at the Health Goddess. Or even just when your dad sat on me. What you do for me all the time, actually."

"Does this mean—" I am scared to say it, almost. "Does this mean you aren't leaving?"

Inkling leans against me. "Bandapat code of honor. I can't leave until that Hetsnickle is well and fully paid. Plus, now that you've got a job, I think my squash worries are over."

I realize: He doesn't owe me.

He *wants* to stay.

He wants to be here, with me, more than he wants a

whole patch full of pumpkins. More than he wants the Halloween Pumpkin-Carving Extravaganza.

"What's for lunch?" Inkling asks.

I look.

My yogurt, a ham sandwich, dried apricots, Cheddar Bunnies, and water. A large yellow apple and a Tupperware of rainbow sprinkles.

All for me to eat in peace.

I open the container and push the sprinkles toward Inkling. "Have some."

The Tupperware lifts, and a small avalanche of sprinkles pours into Inkling's mouth. Then they go invisible. "Thanks," he says, chewing. "Don't mind if I do."

A thing about Inkling is, he hogs whatever food he gets.

A thing about Inkling is, he shows up when you need him.

A thing about me is, I have an invisible friend.

And that means—

Anything could happen next.

Author's Note

Invisible Inkling is set in an imaginary Brooklyn neighborhood—a combination Cobble Hill, Boerum Hill, and Park Slope. The ice-cream shop in the story is inspired by Blue Marble, which has the best strawberry ice cream I've ever tasted. I made up almost all the details of Big Round Pumpkin, but you still might want to learn more about Blue Marble: www.bluemarbleicecream.com. The park, the school, the pizza place, the Thai restaurant, and the health food store—all are based on places I go regularly, even though they've been fictionalized.

WHAT HAPPENS NEXT FOR HANK AND INKLING?

Take a look at an excerpt from

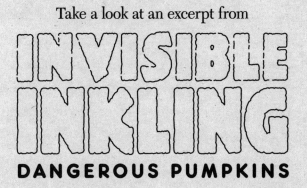

DANGEROUS PUMPKINS

Did You Know There's This Holiday Called Halloween?

A thing about me is, I hate Halloween.

A thing about Inkling is, he never even heard of it until three weeks ago. Then he got crazy excited.

See, bandapats like to eat squash. In fact, they *need* to eat squash. If they don't get it, their fur gets matted and their legs go weak.

Also, they get cranky.

Pumpkins are their favorite.

Problem is, it's not easy to get squash in Brooklyn. Where I live is all brownstones and brick townhouses, little neighborhood shops, restaurants, and traffic. It's

1

part of New York City! There are no pumpkin patches.

I buy what squash I can for Inkling, but I don't have a lot of cash. Also, the guy at the corner market wonders why I spend all my money on large vegetables.

My friend Sasha Chin from downstairs wonders about it, too.

So does Dad.

I told them all I was doing a top secret squash project for Halloween.

That was a lie.

I tell a lot of lies now that Inkling lives with me. Like, I told Dad I had an imaginary friend. And I let everyone think I bit this dirtbug Gillicut at school, when really Inkling bit him. I told my sister, Nadia, I was starting to be allergic to dogs, too. That's because Inkling's afraid of Rootbeer across the hall.

With telling so many lies, you'd think I'd know better than to tell that one about the top secret squash project. Lying that you're doing a big project is extremely dumb. People are going to want to see it. I can't even invent a fake project at the last minute. Inkling's eaten every squash I bought.

I hate being a liar mainly because it's wrong. It makes

me feel bad about myself. But I'll be honest with you: it wouldn't be so hard if I was actually a *good* liar.

Anyway, when Inkling first found out about Halloween, he was all, "Wolowitz! Did you know there's this holiday called Halloween?"

Well, hello?

We'd been playing Blokus in my bedroom. Inkling waved the strategy tip sheet at me. It flapped in the air as if by magic. "Did you know human beings actually hollow out pumpkins and *throw away* cups and cups of squash?" he asked.

"I've heard of that, yeah."

You would not believe how excited he was. I could hear him breathing hard when he talked about it. He didn't even care about the trick-or-treating. Or the candy. Or the special ice-cream flavors.

Now, the Saturday before Halloween weekend, carved pumpkins begin appearing on the stoops of buildings in our neighborhood. Inkling starts heavy breathing when he sees the first one. We're walking down the block, him on my back. He's clutching my shoulders with his claws, he's so hyper.

When we turn the corner, there are six jack-o'-lanterns

clustered on one stoop. Big ones and small ones, grinning wildly. Inkling starts mumbling to himself. "Ooh, pretty pumpkins. Pretty, pretty pumpkins. Hello! You are waiting for Inkling, aren't you? There for my lunch. Yummy, yummy!"

"Excuse me," I say. "Those are not yours."

"Oh yes they are," he says in my ear. "Yummy, yummy. Pretty, pretty."

Inkling is riding on my back because he doesn't like to walk around our neighborhood. There are too many dogs and feet. It's dangerous for a small, invisible person.

We are going to the corner fruit market to buy some radishes and lettuce for my mom. I bought Inkling a squash there yesterday, like I do every Friday when I get paid—but it wasn't a pumpkin. Acorn squashes are a lot cheaper than pumpkins. If I buy an acorn squash, I have enough money left over for candy.

"People carved those jack-o'-lanterns," I tell Inkling. "They're works of art."

"They're abandoned on the street!"

"No, they're not. They're decorations."

"It's like I dreamed Halloween would be. Pumpkins lining the streets of Brooklyn." He starts muttering again. "Yum-yum, pumpkins. Oh, little pumpkins, you are just made of yum, aren't you?" Then louder: "Go on, Wolowitz. Get me one."

"No."

"Get two. Get big ones."

"I'll buy you one at the store, but you can't eat the jack-o'-lanterns on the stoops."

"Buy it."

"I can't now. It's not my own money. I have to buy radishes and lettuce. You have to wait until I get paid."

"Now! Now!"

I reach back and grab Inkling by the scruff of his thick, furry neck. I yank him around and hold him in front of me. I look where I think his eyes are. "You know I don't get paid till Friday," I bark. "You have to control yourself!"

"Hank?" A voice startles me. "Hank, whatcha doing?"

It's Joe Patne, a kid from my class. Standing there with his dad. Looking at me like I'm a crazy person.

Probably Only
Small Ponies, Though

I drop Inkling and pretend to scratch my arm. "Oh, hi, Patne," I say.

"What are you doing?" he asks.

"Buying radishes for my mom. What are you doing?"

"Dad and I are going swimming at the gym on Court Street." He takes his glasses off and digs a pair of goggles from his bag. He puts them on. They make him look like a supervillain, which I like. "What I meant was, why are you yelling at the air?"

Patne and I are kind of friends.

I mean, we were. Kind of.

He went to Science Fellow camp with me and my best friend, Wainscotting, after second grade. I went to his birthday party in third grade and he went to mine. But Patne was out of town all last summer, and when school started again and Wainscotting moved away to Iowa—well. I don't hang around with him anymore.

Why not?

I don't know.

He goes to after-school every day, and I get picked up. Plus, his family moved to Clinton Hill and now he gets to Public School 166 on the subway instead of walking. Still, after-school and geography are not really reasons to stop being friends with a guy.

"Swimming sounds fun," I say.

"But why were you yelling at your hand?"

"I was, ah, speaking of swimming, do you ever think there might be a giant lizard in the swimming pool, even though you know there isn't? Like, you're sure it's lurking in the deep end, the part where the water is cold."

"Not really," says Patne.

"I always think of giant lizards," I say. "Or maybe water snakes. The faint-banded sea snake is insanely poisonous. And the anaconda isn't venomous but it's very huge. It can squeeze ponies to death and eat them."

"No idea what you're talking about," says Patne. "But that's cool about the ponies."

I can't believe he doesn't ever think about creatures lurking in the swimming pool. I mean, I know I have an overbusy imagination, but that was something I thought *everybody* worried about.

At least he's stopped asking why I yelled at my hand.

"Probably only small ponies, though." I say. "Pygmy ponies. I—whoa!"

A jack-o'-lantern rolls across my feet. A large one.

Inkling!

I stop the pumpkin with one foot and smile up at Patne like nothing weird is happening.

"Is that your pumpkin?" he asks.

"No," I say, loudly and meaningfully. "This is *not* my pumpkin. It is not a pumpkin belonging to anyone I know. This is a stranger pumpkin that just rolled off its stoop. We should put it back. It belongs to somebody who cares very much about it."

I lug the pumpkin back to the stoop. It is really, really heavy.

There is a quiet chewing sound. Coming from inside it.
Oh no.

Inkling is eating the stranger pumpkin from inside.
Should I try and talk to Patne like a normal person?
Pretend like it's not happening? Or should I save the
pumpkin by taking off the cap and yanking Inkling out,
which means Patne will think I am crazy?

I whack the pumpkin with my open palm. "This is someone's special jack-o'-lantern!" I say loudly. "It's good to respect our neighbors and their holiday decorations!"

"Hank, I still have no idea what you're talking about," says Patne. "I have to go to the pool now."

"Okay!" I say, slapping the pumpkin again. "Good-bye and have a nice day!"

As soon as Patne's gone, I yank Inkling out and tuck him under my arm like a towel. "You're insulting my dignity," he mutters.

"You lost that a long time ago," I tell him.